The Crying Hour

By Jack Hannigan

"No one ever told me that grief felt so like fear."

— C.S. Lewis

Contents

1 Chapter 1 – The Perfect Day 6
2 Chapter 2 – Nancy 11
   2.1 March 1984 – Present day 11
   2.2 January 1955 14
   2.3 February 1955 17
   2.4 March 1984 – Present day 23
3 Chapter 3 – Jonathan 24
   3.1 June 1967 24
   3.2 October 1965 25
4 Chapter 4 – The Family 29
   4.1 July 1982 29
5 Chapter 5 – Henry 32
   5.1 November 1968 32
6 Chapter 6 – Peacock Street 34
   6.1 March 1984 – Present day 34
7 Chapter 7 – The Incident 44
   7.1 June 1982 44
8 Chapter 8 – The Lunchroom 51
   8.1 March 1984 – Present day 51
9 Chapter 9 – The Funeral 54
   9.1 March 1984 – Present day 54
10 Chapter 10 – The Miracle 59
   10.1 October 1976 59
11 Chapter 11 – The TV Room 63
   11.1 March 1984 – Present day 63
12 Chapter 12 – The Homecoming 68
   12.1 July 1982 68
13 Chapter 13 - The Boys on the beach 74
   13.1 March 1984 – Present day 74
   13.2 July 1931 76
Chapter 14 – The Lost Boy 86
   13.3 March 1977 86
14 Chapter 15 – Fears and Demons 92
   14.1 February 1979 92

- 15 Chapter 16 – The Group Session 95
  - 15.1 March 1984 – Present day 95
- 16 Chapter 17 – The Revelation 104
  - 16.1 July 1982 104
- 17 Chapter 18 – In The End 109
- 18 The Crying Hour - Appendix 116
  - 18.1 Characters: 116
  - 18.2 Timeline 116

1 Chapter 1 – The Perfect Day

"Doesn't Henry look handsome today?" Mary says, head cocked and eyebrows raised in a way that made her cousin Nancy giggle as they used to as schoolgirls. Mary chances a wave at the altar, but her nephew, Henry, stooped and whispering to his father, doesn't notice. "Did you see the bleeding bridesmaids in those dresses? Look like overegged cakes with too much frosting. Wouldn't have caught me dead in that, believe you me, Nancy."

"They look gorgeous, and you know it. You old misery," retorts Nancy. Mary sticks out her tongue and catches Nancy giggle as Henry turns for another furtive glance towards the church entrance.

Mary pulls her good silk handkerchief from her emerald clutch handbag and dabs at Nancy's cheek to stop the tears falling and staining her dress. The laughing and chatting die down, and the two ladies take each other's hands as Nancy shifts herself forward to take her place with her husband. She smiles at her cousin, and they embrace, eyes tightly shut and smiles beaming.

"I reckon I'll be off to my seat, love," Mary whispers into Nancy's ear. She gives her cousin a final squeeze as the congregation turns from informal chatter to solemn dignity. As she turns to go, Nancy pulls her in for a final hug. "We couldn't be prouder. You hear?" Mary's voice is fierce now in Nancy's ear. "That young man has overcome every fecking thing, obstacle after obstacle after all that bother, and he's come out the other side whole and human, and you did that, Nance, you hear? You did that."

Mary pulls away without a backwards glance and brings a row of men to their feet as they compete to escort her to where she would eventually sit, still sobbing uncontrollably without a care of her surroundings. Nancy makes her way to her seat and sees her daughters brushing down their bridesmaid dresses, their flushed faces setting off the light-yellow lace.

They were both still young, Sarah a year older, and Nancy suspected she was leading Emily on her night-time ramblings. Boys would be knocking soon, asking for permission to court, as if they hadn't taken it already. Nancy can´t suppress the swell of pride as she watches them joke with the guests and family.

Nancy spots her husband, Jonathan, so handsome even as he approaches sixty, his reassuring presence at the front of the church, constantly holding court with friends and family, then at the same time doing everything he can to quash his son's nerves as the big moment approaches. Her eyes soften and she smiles as she notices how wonderful he looks in his suit.

Nancy can't help but think to herself how she could never live without him. Her adoration is compelling. He is the kindest and most honest man she has ever met, he is her hero, and he is her eternal love. Nancy, realising how soppy she must seem, blushes and resumes her mother-of-the-groom duties, smiling and nodding at the arriving guests.

Nancy looks back at her son, his increasingly nervous disposition very evident to her, though he tries to hide these jitters with his winsome smile, that smile she had adored her whole life, radiating pure happiness, the unparalleled love linking mother and child.

Henry notices his mother standing, solemn, at the back of the church, visibly emotional, and a tender smile directed to him. She is taking in this moment, absorbing the abundant joy pulsating through the church. He playfully sticks out his tongue at his mother, and she laughs, covering her mouth with her un-gloved hand. The pair smile at each other mischievously as they used to when Henry was a boy, a moment of mutual understanding, the understanding that for them both to get to this very moment had been extremely difficult. They had both played their roles in a long and painful journey, one they had struggled through together.

Henry, realising that the church is now full, taps his watch in recognition of the time. Soon the ceremony would begin. "Come on, Mum," he mimes, waving his hand, beckoning his mother towards him so she can take her position with their family at the front of the church. Nancy moves to the front and takes her place with Jonathan. She looks up at the rafters, old oak beams straddling the space below, then around the quaint little church they had all surprisingly managed to cram into. The sun illuminates the whole building through the arresting and vibrant stained-glass windows on either side of the pews, filling every inch with soft light and vibrant colour. At this moment, Nancy is more content and happier than she has ever been in her life. She closes her eyes for a second, preparing to take a mental snapshot of the day, a memory photo she can keep with her always. Then, her eyes open.

For a second, there is darkness and silence. Nancy looks for the people around her, but everyone is gone. Nancy's immediate thought is that the lights have tripped, but how? It's midday and sunny, she reminds herself, still ascertaining what has happened. Then before she can speak, she is back in the church; everything is normal, but just for a few moments, then the hollow lifeless dark place again; then again, she is back in the church. Her husband is smiling beside her, and people are waiting for the wedding to begin. She wonders if she is having a stroke or a brain aneurysm, the continuous doubt over her wellness lasting for several minutes, several very confusing minutes. Then all of a sudden, the people and the church begin to flicker faster, they fade from Nancy's mind like an old television set with a weak signal, a clear image then a flicker, then nothing, and it repeats, over and over. Still confused, she tries in vain to maintain this life, to maintain the clear image that is her family and friends, the place she is happy.

She looks again to the light and safety of the stained-glass window and the soft beams of light illuminating the people around the church, as she scans the walls and windows looking for a sign or even a moment of realisation to understand what's happening. Nancy's eyes lock on the image of St Michael vanquishing the Devil, majestic and powerful, his foot suppressing the beast below him, spear poised to deal a deadly blow. She focuses on the fear in Satan's eyes and she recognises him; he is holding on to a cliff edge, a pit of unearthly fire waits for him below, she knows he will inevitably fall. And he does, right there, in front of her eyes, he falls from the window beyond the flames to somewhere below the church floor, as Michael lifts his spear in triumphant victory. She is teetering on the ledge of lucidity.

Nancy no longer feels her husband's strong hand in hers. She sees out of the corner of her eyes that Mary and several other guests have disappeared from the bench behind her. Nancy looks at her girls standing beside the altar, but they begin to pale into obscurity, slowly, to begin with, then increasingly, pale and doll-like, heads nodding slowly back and forth with no rhythm or pattern, their faces blurring and eventually becoming even more unidentifiable with every uncomfortable nod. Nancy looks on in horror as their noses and eyes turn to black spots, as if they've been pierced or pricked by a large needle, and the feature that was there has been plucked and squeezed from their pretty faces. Nancy turns to see Henry smile one last time just as his once happy expression warps and his mouth slides across his cheek and falls to his neck, then stops, like a damaged Picasso. Then, almost simultaneously his eyes and nose are swallowed by his head, he is faceless, a ghost. "What in God's name is happening here, Jonathan?" Nancy says in silent fright, turning to see her husband rising like a mist, his face and body evaporating into the rafters.

Nancy's daughters begin to merge into one, their pinhole faces and bodies becoming a pink blob of bodily parts, four arms and legs protruding from the openings in the dresses, then they too, like the others before, evaporate into the rafters. By the time she turns to see Jonathan, he is all but gone. She sees the outline that was his face turn to particles and drift upwards into all the corners of the church, along with the remaining wedding guests.

Nancy's entire family eventually evanesce from her life. Then, the darkness is all she can feel.

Nancy wakes up from the smoke filling her lungs. Where was the church? Where was her family? Where was Henry? Where was the stained-glass window of Michael vanquishing the Devil? She had been there only moments ago. Was it real? Tears stream from her eyes, but she opens them and sees fire all around her. She is in bed, unable to move, but the pain she feels both physically and emotionally is more than she can bear. She longs for the end, and to live in this everlasting moment with her family, but it is gone, and she is alone.

These are Nancy's last thoughts as her mind flits between a dream world and reality, her life slowly and painfully drifting away. She is on the cusp of death, and it can't come too soon. The fire rages all around the place where she is lying. She cannot move, and her attempts to scream are quelled by the smoke in her lungs. The figure of a man moves towards her. "Jonathan," Nancy croaks, the smoke that fills her throat hindering any articulation of words. She feels strong arms wrap themselves around her, and her body elevated from her bed, then nothing.

2 Chapter 2 – Nancy

2.1 March 1984 – Present day

Nancy Blake lies awake, her eyes transfixed on the high ceiling of her dorm, the angles of the room expanding upward to the dark wooden beams above her. It is quiet aside from the wind blowing eerily down the empty corridor just outside her door. "Another day," she says to herself through her morning yawn and stretch, raising her arms to the ceiling. She feels her bones cracking in each shoulder, then in her back, the relief spreading through her body.

The light begins to filter in through the sash window beside her. She can see the dust dancing in the beam rising and falling on her white pillow. She looks over at her alarm clock. '5.58 a.m.' It flashes annoyingly, Nancy's eyes squinting at the blurry fluorescent lines making up the numbers. She is still sleepy. It's far too early to get up, she thinks to herself, and lies back on the bed, eyes once again to the ceiling. None of the nurses ever sleep well on a night shift.

The time from 10 pm until 11 pm is what the nurses have rather coldly dubbed 'the crying hour'. This is by far the worst time of the day for Nancy and the other nurses. It is the time when they must put the patients to bed, to lock them in solitude, some restricted to their beds with straps, many bound in jackets like animals, all with only their thoughts, memories, and nightmares to keep them company. Agonising cries are heard from the depths of souls. Screams echo through parallel lives that could have been. Mothers, fathers, sons, daughters, husbands, wives, and lovers are all screamed for by one patient or another. Some long to be close to their loved ones once again, some the opposite, cursing those people they loved the most, for abandoning them at the hospital, for washing their hands of an inconvenience that had become more than they could live with, for the abuse that had been inflicted upon them, for leaving them alone on this Earth, alone and forgotten.

Nancy would often hear the screams that echoed up and down the Georgian corridors throughout the night. Some of the patients were trapped in their own minds, living ghosts, imprisoned in a world they could not escape, except through the eventual release of death. But many of the patients were committed due to the neglect and shame of family members and would have been perfectly capable of living in the outside world with just a small amount of help and adjustment. All were victims of an unaccepting and unkind time when people could be passed off to these types of places, and then conveniently forgotten about.

Aside from these nightly disturbances, Nancy's shift had very few incidents. That meant she had gotten a reasonable night's rest before her last shift of the week, a much-needed Friday had come along, and she would not let anything ruin her day.

Nancy is a wife, mother, and nurse. These are the three things she values above anything else in this life, all the things that make her happy, and she is good at them. Now in her early forties, she is still attractive enough to be noticed, but as she gazes at the mirror each morning, she notices new lines and wrinkles appearing every day. She grows increasingly aware that age is relentlessly catching up with her. She is a petite woman with a slim figure, something she has always been proud and ashamed of in equal measure. While her colleagues gain weight or fluctuate from large to small, Nancy has remained pretty much the same. She has a kind face with pretty features—deep brown eyes and a button nose. Her thick blonde hair is always immaculate, neat and motionless above her shoulders.

Nancy is, for all intents and purposes, the typical working housewife of her generation. She is the mother and the wife, the anchor, and the heart of her family. But buried beneath the layers of the makeup that cover her pretty face, there is an altogether different person. Once the mask is removed every night, we see a woman worn out from striving to keep her family together, always being there for them through all the turmoil and strife. Peacock Street Psychiatric Hospital has been her place of work for 14 years, and these years of long and tiring nights have taken their toll on Nancy. The wear and tear of time are unforgiving, taking her youth and beauty, slowly but surely stripping away her confidence, the reality confirmed with every passing reflection, reminding her of this evolutionary curse that continues her decay, one day at a time.

Nancy had always run-on nervous energy; this was very evident from her disposition. She would often scratch her skin and crack her knuckles; her eyes would flicker like hummingbird wings when she was listening intently to something. Some people, including staff members, found this quite disconcerting, and many of the younger nurses would giggle and make fun of her behind her back. Nancy attempted to ignore them, but cruelty and mockery can hit people hard. Nancy did not show it, but the comments hurt her deeply.

This morning, Nancy lies in bed for a while. She thinks about nothing and everything while allowing her mind to adjust to the morning, like a computer rebooting. Her shaking hand reaches for the red box sitting on her bedside table. Quickly and unsteadily, she lights her cigarette and gently inhales before exhaling slowly, watching, with a degree of satisfaction, the beautiful but deadly smoke swirling within the cavernous dorm room of the hospital, the same room she has slept in once a fortnight for the last 14 years.

Nancy has smoked heavily and compulsively since she was a young girl. When her parents were out of the house, she would steal cigarettes from their secret stash, which they always kept in a biscuit tin above the food cupboard in their kitchen. She would then make her escape, running to catch the number 14 bus to the other side of town, where she would meet with her best friend Hannah in Whitland Park. On arrival, Nancy would share the spoils of her heist with her friend. They would both unwind on the freshly cut lawn in the centre of the park, eyes to the sky, the gentle touch of short grass tickling their backs and necks as they stared at the clouds and birds hovering above them, heads adjacent so they could be as close as physically possible to each other while they chatted. These two best friends talked and laughed without a care in the world as they passed cigarettes back and forth. Hours passed like the clouds above them as they talked about anything and everything they could think of. Time did not exist in those moments, but those moments defined that time for them both.

Nancy would often think back to those days, remembering how she would laugh with her best friend. She'd think of Hannah's rosy cheeks and her naughty sense of humour. But with many happy memories we often have the subliminal trigger of a bad memory to accompany these treasured and sacred thoughts, a memory we hide and push back to the underworld of our minds. It is something we can't easily shake or remove once awakened, and Nancy is no exception.

2.2 JANUARY 1955

It is a Tuesday, not long after Nancy's 14th birthday, an important birthday for any teenage girl. On this day, she had been to the cinema for the first time, as well as receiving an artist's easel, paints, and paper from her grandmother. It had been one of the best days of Nancy's short existence to date.

"I am a young woman now, and an aspiring artist to boot," Nancy thinks to herself as she prepares to head out and meet her friend. On this Tuesday Nancy returns home from school slightly earlier than normal, and as per usual, she is heading out later to meet her best friend Hannah in the park. The earliness of her arrival is opportune, as her parents are both working and there is no one at home. Nancy seizes her opportunity to reward her early homecoming with her textbook great cigarette robbery. Nancy strategically reaches for the prize, one knee on the kitchen unit, the other foot tiptoeing on the beige kitchen lino, this stance keeping her precariously balanced as she steadies herself with her left hand. Her right hand reaches up and then rummages over the top of the corner cupboard to where she usually finds her reward. To her dismay, on this occasion, she finds nothing other than a few loose matches, but no tin and no cigarettes. "Oh shit, the tin hasn't been refilled, I can't believe it!" she mutters to herself in disbelief, still perched in a precarious position on the kitchen unit. She stops to consider her next move. "Hannah won't be very happ..." She stops speaking, and her heart skips a beat as she is disturbed by a sudden noise. It is the kitchen door opening and closing behind her, and then quiet.

Nancy knows this is not good, and her palms start to sweat. She immediately drops to the floor with a thud. Her dad has returned from work early. He had not been feeling well all week and could not continue with his day at the factory, so he had decided to take the rest of the week off. He stands for a second, confused, trying to deduce what his daughter had been doing on the kitchen counter, why a look of guilt is covering her face like a dog caught in the pantry. Her wide eyes and her ruby cheeks give the game away to her father.

Nancy notices the rage slowly rising inside him as he realises what his daughter had been up to. His anger engulfs his mind and body, his fists clenched so tight his hands and knuckles are a mixture of white and red. For a moment, the room is still, and Nancy is frozen, a mixture of shock and fear surging through her. As yet, she has not quite fully turned to face this man she knows so well but does not recognise at this moment. All at once, he charges at her, and before Nancy realises what is happening, he punches her hard on the top of her back, right between her shoulder blades, directly below her neck. She assumes he has hit her with all his strength because before she can say a word to him, her body has slammed violently against the floor. She does not have the time or reflexes to use her hands to break the fall; it is instant and brutal, and her face and body hit the floor simultaneously, causing a pain she has never experienced before. The pain starts to circle and spread inside her torso, leaving her breathless and panicked. She fears she may die there and then on her kitchen floor. It feels like the punch has somehow ripped the lungs out from inside of her and broken her back all at the same time. Winded and bruised, she lies there for a few seconds, gasping in vain for air. She attempts to cry, but the lack of oxygen stops her, again and then again. Until finally, sweet relief comes, the air fills her lungs again, and she is able to sit up and after a moment stand, albeit shakily.

As Nancy eventually finds her feet, she looks over at her father, who has retreated a few yards away from the incident. He is sitting at the kitchen table with his head in his hands, slowly rocking back and forth, over and over, clearly contemplating what has just happened. Nancy's father, shaking and ashamed, looks up at his battered daughter. "I'm sorry Nancy, I'm so very sorry… I'm… I'm so very sorry, I don't seem to have control anymore... There's something wrong with me and I can't seem to get back to normal. I don't feel like myself anymore. I'm so deeply sorry, my darling. How can you ever forgive me now?" Here is not the Titan that had just struck her; this man, pale and sobbing, is now reduced to a shadow of the monster who attacked her moments before.

Nancy had noticed her father's behaviour become increasingly erratic over the previous weeks in the lead-up to the cigarette incident. He had been prone to unprovoked rage, spells of hysteria, and catatonic depression. This was a man Nancy knew as proud and gentle, her go-to person for any issues she had, and any issues anyone else had for that matter, both friends and relatives alike. A man who would cuddle and kiss her before school every day, then repeat the ritual when she returned home in the evening.

As Nancy stands over her father this fateful day, she recognises the man she knows so well. Her father has reappeared, and the monster is gone. "It's ok, Dad, honestly. I know I shouldn't have tried to take the cigarettes. It was really silly of me, it's my own stupid fault." There is a moment of calm as Nancy observes her father's broken pride. He looks at his daughter, tears welling up in his bloodshot eyes. Nancy walks into his arms and rests her head on his blue-striped shirt. She feels his warm chest on her cheek as he sobs for several minutes, unable to stop. The groans of sorrow and regret ring through the room. This normally gentle man is unable to forget what he has just done to the daughter whom he loves more than anything in this world.

That afternoon was one of Nancy's last significant memories of her father. He had, unbeknownst to himself or anyone else, been living with a metastatic brain tumour for several years, refusing to go to a doctor about his headaches. A kind but stubborn man, he'd say to his family, "I'll be ok, obviously superheroes don't get sick, isn't that right, Nancy?" He would wink at her and flex his muscles, and she in return would wink back and giggle at his acknowledgement of their private joke. After the incident with the cigarettes, he did not go back to work, and he died ten days later, in his armchair, in the family sitting room. Nancy was the one who discovered him, cold and still. Two streams of dark red blood had run from his nose over his lips onto his blue-striped shirt.

2.3 FEBRUARY 1955

The funeral is attended by many people, family, friends and work colleagues from far and wide. Nancy arrives with her mum, and they both do their duties, chatting with friends and relatives, tears and smiles, shared memories, for this man loved by many, a man whose pain has now ceased, so he can now rest in peace.

Nancy leaves the church and begins chatting with some of the congregation, directing people to the house for refreshments, as she was told to do by her mother. While thanking the vicar for the service, she notices a woman talking with her mother. She is dressed in black and purple and has long wiry grey hair to her waist. She is short and old, her eyes are dark and haunting, but Nancy notices she has a sweet smile. Take away this smile, and this woman would not look out of place in a horror movie or being burnt at the stake three centuries earlier. Nancy, after a moment, recognises with surprise that this woman is her maternal grandmother and, in that recognition, she remembers this lady visiting the family home when she was younger. Her father would call her 'The Gypsy Woman', but her father and his mother-in-law got on very well as far as Nancy remembered. Nancy's mother, Grace, on the other hand, did not like her mother, or her way of life.

Nancy remembered times when her grandmother had visited. She would spend much of her time outside in the garden, sleeping in a makeshift tent made from old sheets and blankets. She would live in her own little world, often talking to the trees and the flowers. She would sometimes dance around the lawn blowing kisses at the sky, singing old Gaelic songs and picking herbs for different remedies she would concoct in an old pan over a fire. More disturbingly, she would also sometimes speak to things people couldn't see, as though she were conversing with ghosts. She would sometimes laugh, cry, or both when involved in these spiritual conversations. Nancy remembered finding this very funny. Looking at a woman talking to an empty stool is very amusing for a five-year-old, and both Nancy and her father would often watch from the window in fits of giggles. Nancy's mum, unlike Nancy and her father, over time, would become increasingly angry at her mother's actions and eccentricities.

The last time Nancy had seen her grandmother was around ten years before her father's funeral. She had been visiting the family again, but for some reason, Nancy remembered on this occasion that her behaviour had been particularly strange and erratic, which had scared Nancy slightly. Her grandmother had repeatedly cupped her head in her hands when her parents were out and had made her dance around the garden while she recited strange words in Gaelic to her granddaughter. Though Nancy tried hard, she could never remember what her grandmother had said to her.

That following evening, her parents returned home from a shopping trip and were chatting with her grandmother in the kitchen while Nancy played with her dolls in the living room next door. Nancy remembered suddenly hearing voices begin to rise in the room next to her. She heard shrieks of rage from her mother and the words "Get out! Get out, you evil old bitch! Don't you ever step into my house again!" Then a door slammed. This was the last time she had seen her grandmother. Until today.

As Nancy observes her mother and grandmother talking privately, she is surprised by how calm they both are and how amicably they are talking, considering what had happened the last time they were together. They spot Nancy looking at them and walk over.

"Hello, Grandmother, how are you? It's very lovely to see you again," Nancy exclaims. Her grandmother is delighted by the sight of her only granddaughter after all these years and hugs her tightly.

"It's so lovely to see you too, my dear, you're a young woman now, just look at yourself, b'jesus! So grown up so you are." Nancy smiles and blushes at her grandmother's comment.

"And I'm sorry about your father so I am" she continues, her voice breaking slightly. "He was a wonderful man. I was incredibly fond of him, so ye hear."

Tears start to form around her eyes, and she takes a tissue from her bag to dry them. She looks to Nancy's mother who is nearby chatting to another funeral guest.

"I must go now, dear, but know that I love you both dearly and remember, Nancy, ye must always remember what I taught ye… níl aon bhás ann ach athrú an domhain." There they were—those words she had heard so long ago. "Use it wisely, use it carefully," her grandmother says softly into her ear, then kisses her granddaughter and then her daughter, and hurries towards the gate of the cemetery. Nancy notices her grandmother look back once, tears still in her eyes.

Nancy is left confused. "Mum, what just happened here? Why did she come and then leave suddenly like that?"

Grace stands for a moment, watching her mother finally disappear. She looks up and smiles at the white clouds passing slowly overhead.

"She loved your dad, Nancy, but she knew what was wrong. She knew all along what would happen, every detail. She knew she had to tell me as her daughter to try and spare me the pain… I understand now she didn't feel she had a choice."

Grace holds Nancy's hands, still looking to the passing clouds now beginning to darken.

"When I was a girl, maybe 13 or 14, I don't remember exactly how old now, your grandmother told me a story, a story I will never forget. One night after a bottle of whiskey or two—which happened quite frequently I will say—she came into my room late one night, sat next to me on the bed but said nothing. I was awake, but I pretended I was asleep, as I did sometimes. She knew, though, she always knew when I was awake. She put her hand on my back and asked me a very strange question. She asked me whether I'd ever felt things in my dreams, whether I could touch and feel the world beyond this one…

I said no, obviously. I was confused. I didn't really know what she was talking about, to be honest.

She sat quietly for a while, rubbing my back, and occasionally stroking my hair. Though I could smell the alcohol exuding from her body, I didn't mind her being there. It was comforting. She was never a nurturing, loving mother, so it was nice for me… Anyway. I lay silent for a while, listening to her draw breath and exhale softly. Then she began speaking to me. She started to tell me a story.

She said that when she was 18, living back in Ireland, she had begun having nightmares, about people, about grief, about heartache, about death. Nightmares so real she swore she could stroke the figures' faces, feel their warm breath on her skin and touch the light raindrops falling from the sky. Generally, the nightmares were about people she had never met, but sometimes, very occasionally, she would see the town folk, the people she would encounter and socialise with every day; she would see their dark secrets and their tragic futures. After a while, the nightmares finally stopped, and she eventually forgot these terrorising dreams. Until one night.

She told me, one particular evening, she'd had dinner with her mother and brother, Andrew, as usual, and they had been joined by his girlfriend Orla, who was three months pregnant. This was not something that was well accepted in a small Catholic town, as you can imagine, so they had to keep it from everyone they knew. Thankfully, Andrew and Orla had planned to marry the following month, so all would be well. The family and Orla ate the fish that Andrew had caught that day on his fishing boat and drank the local whiskey. It had been a pleasant evening for all. They had talked about names for the baby, and whom it would resemble once it was born.

My mother said that she had fallen asleep with ease that night. She had been worried about Andrew and Orla, but now that they were to be married, that worry had diminished. As she fell into a deep slumber, she saw them in her dream. She saw them happy, laughing with a little girl, both kneeling, washing her tiny face and curly brown hair with a flannel. The girl was splashing in the tin bathtub they owned. It was beautiful. They were beautiful. She repeated this several times before she began to sob. I seem to remember I had never heard her cry before then."

Grace stops for a second and then directs her gaze to the church beyond Nancy, a look of contempt directed towards the house of God they are standing next to. She continues with the story, gathering the details from this memory that Nancy cannot quite fathom why is being shared with her.

Grace continues, "Then, all at once, Andrew vanishes into thin air, then Orla as well, and the child is left alone. She wails and wails, standing in her bath, her naked body shifting from one side to the other, searching the corners of the room for her mother and father, her haunting cries echoing throughout the room.

My mother said she ran from the house to search for her brother, but it was dark, and she had no torch. She first ran through the fields to the town but could find no one, every street empty. Then she ran to the docks, searching relentlessly but in vain, shouting his name, and searching every fishing boat moored to the jetty. In her frenzied state, she slips and hits her head on the hard mossy timbers of the dock and then slips off the side into the gloomy water below. Darkness engulfs her as she sinks to the seabed. When she finally opens her eyes, the water is murky, but she sees them, lying side by side on the bed of the ocean, anchors and lobster nets surrounding them, Andrew and Orla, pale and lifeless, the moonlight illuminating their bodies in the shallow water.

When she awoke the next day, she ran to the dock as fast as she could and begged Andrew not to go to sea that day. She pleaded and cried until he finally gave in and let his first mate and skipper man the boat that day. When they returned, Andrew's shipmates, I mean, he gave his first mate, Gordon, and cabin boy Patrick a shilling and sent them to the pub as a reward for their hard work, while Andrew stayed and cleaned the boat, a job usually reserved for his first mate.

There, somewhere around seven in the evening, Andrew slipped on the dock. He cut his head open on the edge of his boat and fell into the water, sinking to the bottom of the gloomy ocean, only the setting sun and the seagulls there to witness his final moments.

A month after Mary was born, still overcome with grief, Orla killed herself in the same spot, throwing herself into the icy waters where her love had tragically drowned seven months earlier. "Those words that haunt you Nancy, that you always wanted to know, níl aon bhás ann ach athrú an domhain…

There is no death, only the change of worlds."

2.4 MARCH 1984 – PRESENT DAY

As Nancy finishes her cigarette, she looks over at the picture of her family and thinks for a moment about her husband and children, what they were doing that morning. She thinks of them all together sitting around their dining table at home, laughing and joking with each other. She thinks about how much she misses them. She thinks about their holidays at the seaside, cleaning the children's and her husband's faces after eating large ice creams with Flake and strawberry sauce. She thinks about kissing her children goodnight after their bedtime time story. And she thinks about how she would laugh later with her husband in bed about his day at work. Nancy thinks about how proud she was of Jonathan for his achievements. He had risen from a reel boy to become a producer at the BBC. She smiled at the thought of seeing her wonderful family that evening and spending a long relaxing weekend with them after her last shift of the week.

3 CHAPTER 3 – JONATHAN

3.1 JUNE 1967

The morning sun presented its friendly head from out over the tiles of Nancy's quiet little suburban, semi-detached home. Her little street was attractive; some may go as far as to say it was a suburban cliché. Trees arched over from each side of the narrow avenue, forming a branched arch along the mile-long stretch of road. Then when spring would eventually come around, these cherry blossoms would bloom, and the street would be awash with pinks all along the mile stretch.

"What a perfect environment to bring up a family," Nancy hinted to her husband as they stood outside their new house, an aura of happiness emanating from her very being.

"A wedding and new house is a lot to take in, Nancy, but I have to say I've never been happier, darling", Jonathan said with both contentment and an undertone of apprehension. Nancy was oblivious to both the comment and the tone of her fiancé, as she dreamt of future events and the prospective family life she had craved for so long with her adoring husband.

Jonathan Blake and Nancy White had been married the previous Saturday at St. Peter's church, followed by their reception, which had been held at Jonathan's parents' house. A perfect day was had by all who attended. There had been bunting and cake and then late-night dancing on the lawn, followed by a two-day honeymoon in the Cotswolds.

The following week, after a short stay with Jonathan's parents, Nancy and Jonathan moved into their little new house they had been so excited about. Nancy got straight to work on the spare room, preparing for the next stage of their married lives, hoping but at the time still unaware that soon their lives would be occupied by a new member of the family.

3.2 OCTOBER 1965

Nancy had met Jonathan at a party where they had been introduced by their mutual friend Miriam Van Furth. Neither Nancy nor Jonathan really liked Miriam, but rather coincidentally, they had both decided at the last minute to attend her birthday celebrations. Miriam had been Nancy's school friend and was now studying with Jonathan on his media course at university. Jonathan had reluctantly gone on a date with Miriam after they had worked together on a presentation about semiotics in the media. Not long into the date, he very quickly realised that not only was he not interested in Miriam, but that she was not a particularly nice person and could be rather rude, so he made his excuses and left. Jonathan had gone to the party knowing that she now had a boyfriend, so he would not be subjected to her very conspicuous passive-aggressive behaviour towards him for snubbing her after their date.

There were not many guests, but the apartment was small, forcing everyone to stand close to absolute strangers. This is how Jonathan and Nancy's paths crossed. Within moments of meeting Jonathan, Nancy was in love, although she didn't realise it at the time because she had never felt it before, a sort of first-sight type of love that is there, but not realised or understood till later.

"Oh, I am sorry," Nancy mumbles into her wine without looking up, after turning and elbowing Jonathan in the back. Swallowing the dregs of her drink and turning slightly to see his face, her stomach sinks and she lifts her palm to her mouth, realising she has accidentally spilt red wine all over his brown tweed jacket. Nancy tries her best to hide her embarrassment, but the mortified look on her face is all too apparent. Jonathan smiles at her, a smile you want to be yours for your whole life.

"Well, at least you've given me the chance to talk to you. Don't worry about the jacket," he pauses and then whispers with one eyebrow raised, "actually, it isn't mine." He laughs at his own reply, trying to put Nancy at ease, but this only causes Nancy's stomach to fill with butterflies and she struggles to find a reply. Jonathan stops and takes note of Nancy's shyness but continues. "I'm going to head to the kitchen, if you'd like another drink? I fear if one of these cigarettes falls on Miriam's turquoise faux leather sofa, we've all had it." Nancy smiles at him, finally composing herself, and they retreat to the kitchen together.

"Again, I'm really sorry about your jacket, or I mean whosever it belongs to, but if I'm being honest," Nancy pauses as she feels the alcohol kick in, calming her nerves, "I think I may have done you a favour." Her joke makes Jonathan laugh in a way that is both loud and infectious. Jonathan's laugh had a surprisingly calming effect on Nancy; and she couldn't wait to hear it again.

After taking a decent bottle of red wine from the secret stash Miriam had rather sneakily saved for her favourite guests, Nancy and Jonathan find a spot on the windowsill where they can sit without being disturbed. They spend the rest of the evening nestled there in the corner of Miriam's contrived Art Deco apartment, as if no one else was in the room, chatting about the world and beyond, and how Miriam had become even more of a bitch since meeting her theatre director boyfriend, a subject they both found extremely amusing.

As the party dies down, Nancy and Jonathan mutually decide to leave. Jonathan offers to walk Nancy home so they can continue their conversation en route. Nancy is happy to agree to the suggestion. She talks passionately about her nursing, what she has been learning at college, what she wants to do when she gets qualified, and her drive to help people suffering from mental illnesses. The impact of her father's death and the preceding decline of his mental health had lit a spark in Nancy and given her this desire to help suffering people who could not control the sadness and darkness of their minds. Jonathan, not really knowing enough about the subject, continues listening intently to this pretty young woman as if there were no place in the universe he would rather be. As well as sharing the same sense of humour, he also admires her empathy and compassion for others.

Nancy thinks to herself how very handsome Jonathan is. Maybe not what others might consider attractive, but he has some appeal, there is no question, she assures herself. His skin is smooth and fair, and he has big blue eyes, a rugged beard and mid-length auburn hair. Six foot one and slim, he has height on his side as well.

As they walk steadily towards her little flat, Nancy finds she cannot keep her eyes off her handsome new acquaintance. Each time she tries to look elsewhere, she always finds herself looking back into those piercing blue eyes and perfectly shaped lips. It is like an addiction, a pure uncontrollable attraction she had never felt before. Nancy, now increasingly aware of her own loquacious behaviour, has become quieter and observes that Jonathan has become slightly more nervous, although she can see he is desperately trying to hide it. She rightly assumes it is because they are on the home stretch to her flat, and this makes her smile. His coyness has put her at ease with him and made her even more attracted to him. She touches the top of his hand very gently, pulling him closer to her. They stop and turn slowly in tandem, finally facing each other hand in hand. The street is silent, aside from the mild buzz from the white streetlamp overhead, a spotlight capturing a perfect moment.

He carefully touches her cheek, running his hands down her neck to her back and pulling her into his arms. Nancy closes her eyes, awash with excitement. She takes a breath and exhales slowly, opening her eyes to make sure she isn't dreaming. Jonathan is looking longingly at her. He is so close to her that their noses almost touch, but not quite.

"I know we've only just met Nancy, but I think... No! That came out wrong, sorry, let me start again." Jonathan stops to compose himself for a second. "I know you're by far the most beautiful thing I've ever seen in my entire life," says Jonathan quietly. Nancy smiles; she knows these words are as sincere and as heartfelt as love should be. Anticipating their first kiss, she prepares herself, but before she can take another breath he whispers more quietly and gently than she can imagine. "I will never forget this night." The pair then kiss on the pavement outside her home, a moment frozen in time, a moment Nancy will never forget, and then without saying another word they walk up the path to Nancy's little house and through her front door, both smiling and laughing, and not for a second taking their eyes off one another.

It is only the following morning that Nancy realises she has never before had a casual sexual encounter after a first meeting. She in truth had never liked anyone enough, but as she watches Jonathan sleep beside her, she knows this is not casual. It is something much bigger, something different. From that moment, he does not leave her side until the day he dies.

4 Chapter 4 – The Family

4.1 July 1982

This Saturday morning, Nancy awoke especially early for a weekend. Her body tingled with excitement and nerves. Jonathan turned over, his eyes adjusting to the light of the morning, feeling the vibrations of his wife's twitching leg through the mattress. Nancy stared pensively at nothing. Her brain was working overtime and different thoughts came and went like rollercoasters through her mind.

"Everything's going to be fine, sweetheart. Please don't worry too much," Jonathan mumbled through a morning yawn. His crooked smile followed closely behind as he lifted his head from the pillow. Nancy smiled back nervously as she moved her pillow upright onto her baby blue headboard and leant back, resting her head on the top of the pillow in order to look at the magnolia ceiling. She let out a deep sigh, trying to compose herself.

"We get our boy home today, Nancy. We finally get him home," Jonathan said with mild enthusiasm, but the apprehension was clear in Nancy's eyes, and she knew her husband sensed it. This man had been through so much, yet remained positive despite everything.

"Yes sweetheart, I know, we'd better get up and get the girls ready for him. They'll be excited to see him too," she finally responded. As Nancy was dressing, she heard a little voice come from behind her.

"Mummy, Daddy, is Henry home today? We cannot wait to see him!" said Emily, Jonathan and Nancy's youngest daughter, who appeared out of nowhere like a little fairy, finding her way into her parents' room without her parents even noticing her, quietly waiting for her moment to announce her arrival. She jumped enthusiastically onto her parents' bed and started to bounce up and down on the mattress.

"Yes, my darling, this is the day, today we become a family again." Nancy responded with an assuring smile.

Of Nancy's three children, Emily is the youngest. She and her sister Sarah are 14 months apart and look extremely alike to the point they are often mistaken for twins. Nancy and Jonathan had not intended to have any more children after Sarah, but these things happen. Emily had been conceived on a drunken night fuelled by whiskey and beer, after a birthday party for Jonathan's uncle. The couple had been on holiday in Scotland visiting family, and after getting caught up in the moment, the inevitable had happened. Sarah had just been born four months before the holiday, and after the initial shock, Nancy was thrilled. Both of her girls are the apple of her eye, blonde, bonnie, polite, and fun in nature. They are a pleasure for anyone who meets them.

As Nancy made breakfast for her two girls, a boiled egg, toast, and some chopped banana, she was distracted by thoughts of Henry. "How will he cope at home? Has it been too long?" As she turned to retrieve the toast from the toaster an egg slipped out her hand and fell to the floor. "Oh, how silly of me!" Nancy bleated as she returned to the real world.

"Don't worry, Mummy." Sarah could sense her mum's unusual mood. "I'll clean-up for you. No need to worry." Then, grabbing a cloth from the sink, she got to work wiping the egg from around her mother's feet. Nancy smiled.

"Thank you, darling. You are a good girl." Nancy continued with her preparations for breakfast, her mind still a million miles away.

She had visited Henry so many times. Generally, he was good, and the boy she knew he could be, amiable and exuberant. She worshipped him unconditionally, but there had been bad days when she had visited him. She had seen unprovoked rage, moments of violence, rancorous silences, tears, and glimpses of madness. These, however, were nothing compared to the hurt caused by the things he said while in these states. She had neither the heart nor the courage to tell her husband some of his most outrageous and violent comments; his hopes were so high. Nancy could not disabuse him after the torturous time leading up to the awful incident that had caused the breakup of her beloved family.

5 Chapter 5 – Henry

5.1 November 1968

As Nancy looked down at her son, two weeks premature and the smallest, most beautiful, tiny human being she had ever seen, she could not help but smile. She shed tear after tear. Nothing and no one had prepared her for this ineffable happiness. Her husband was beside her, equally as emotional and in love with their son. Her pregnancy was surprisingly easy for a first child, and Jonathan waited on her hand and foot throughout so she would want for nothing. Even the final stages were quick and without too much distress, as far as births go. This day was something both Nancy and Jonathan had dreamed about since they'd met, a tiny symbol of the love they shared.

The hospital was busy, and nurses came and went, checking that mother and baby are ok. The day was pleasant for November. A dim sun shone down on a frosty car park outside the second-floor hospital window. Jonathan wiped away the condensation on the inside to get a better view and showed his son his first look at what lies beyond the hospital ward. The baby in his arms looked out upon the new day, eyes wide, exploring this new world. After a long night of watching his wife and baby sleep in his arms, Jonathan began to feel tired and gave his son back to Nancy, who was now awake and rested. He retreated to the cafeteria for a coffee, leaving Nancy alone with her son.

Nancy and Jonathan had been toying with names since they were told the wonderful news some seven months earlier. They had changed their minds at least 10 or 12 times but were still unsure. Finally, they had narrowed it down to Henry or Stuart, after their respective grandfathers. Jonathan had told Nancy that the decision was hers, and she would know when he arrived.

She looked down at this tiny naked boy, overcome with something deeper than love. His fingers gently explored her face, he gently touched her nose and hair and then moved down to her mouth and across her lips, his eyes wide and curious, experiencing the life around him for the first time. Nancy began to weep as a burning thought entered her mind. She leant over carefully and whispers to her new-born son, "I will protect you; I will shield you from all the evils this world has to inflict and impose. I will do this always, and I will love you unconditionally and forever, my dear beautiful little Henry."

6 CHAPTER 6 – PEACOCK STREET

6.1 MARCH 1984 – PRESENT DAY

Andrea had called in sick. Nancy had taken the initial call and kindly offered to cover her shift. She figured the children were at school and her husband was at work all day, so she could make some extra money. Perhaps she could treat them over the weekend, maybe a day trip to the south coast, some ice cream, and a pub lunch. "What a perfect day and just what we need," she mused to herself.

In the 14 years Nancy worked at Peacock Street Hospital, she had grown extremely popular and accumulated many friends, especially among the older nurses whom she had worked with for many years. She always tried to look her best and helped everyone out as and where she could, although this kind-natured approach had led her into trouble on several occasions. Some nurses, particularly the younger newer girls, would occasionally rather unfairly guilt her into covering their shifts. Their excuses were often that they didn't feel well, or they were having some 'lady issues', and sometimes they were quite blatant, saying that their boyfriend was in, town and they needed Nancy to cover so they could go out dancing. When Nancy tried to refuse the request, saying that she wanted to spend the evening with her family, they would question her friendship "Oh Nancy, I thought we were friends!" or "Oh, but you did it for Liz last week, why not me?" Full of guilt, Nancy would generally oblige (albeit reluctantly) if there wasn't anything overly important happening in her life. This type of friendship of convenience was not the case with Andrea. Nancy and Andrea were close friends, perhaps even best friends, despite their 15-year age gap, although they never really admitted it.

Andrea had told Nancy about the job at Peacock Street when they met on a course about dealing with suicidal patients. Nancy had only just finished college and was deciding what her next move would be. Andrea had put in a good word with the manager, a stout and direct woman with a surprisingly gentle nature named Virginia. Andrea also helped Nancy with her application and final interview and was so proud when she got the job. Because of this generous help from Andrea, Nancy was forever grateful to her friend.

Nancy knew Andrea had been ill for a while, so she was happy to cover for her. Andrea had always been so kind; she was a great friend and colleague, and Nancy thought the world of her. She had also become increasingly worried about her. Andrea had missed a lot of workdays and was looking thin and frail, which she had put down to stress. Little did Nancy know that the phone call she had received that morning would be, sadly, one of the last times she would speak to her friend.

Nancy put on her uniform and applied a small amount of makeup. She was early, so after making her bed, she sat a while planning what she would do with her time off, going through a mental to-do list of everything she knew she had to do that day.

- clean out the spare room
- buy groceries, including ingredients for their Sunday roast
- take the girls out for new school shoes
- meet her husband for lunch in town.

"Perfect!" she whispered, pleased with herself. A smile of satisfaction and contentment appeared on her face as she sat staring over the sill of her window. The view from her room was of the acre-long hospital garden, just a narrow country lane leading to the road, and a solitary ash tree. While she looked outside, Nancy observed the brown leaves fluttering in the wind, the frost resting on the green grass and the glint of the winter sun. Although simple, this made for an idyllic view. "I wish the garden always looked like this," Nancy thought as she rested her forehead on the windowpane. As she walked towards the door, she glanced at her family portrait, smiled, and walked out. There to greet her was her colleague and friend Val.

"Gooood morning Nancy, did you sleep well, my dear?" Val enthusiastically asked Nancy before she had a chance to shut the door behind her.

"Like a log, Valerie, obviously," Nancy replied sardonically. This was an inside joke among the nurses. None of them slept well between the hourly checks they performed once the crying hour had finally stopped. They smiled at each other and proceeded to the dining room.

Nancy had her usual breakfast, a poached egg on a slice of toast, with a small coffee. She conversed with her colleagues, mainly about celebrity gossip and discussed the latest stories in Hollywood and the exploits of the royals, but the girls had all protested for a pay raise the previous week, and eventually won their appeal, so there was a different feel about the place. Nancy couldn't put her finger on it, so assumed it was the aftermath of this. The other nurses would often sit chatting about family and complaining about their husbands and partners, until Mary McKinnock, the head nurse, dispersed the women to their various duties of the day. While the other nurses would take pleasure in criticising their respective partners, Nancy did not utter a single bad word about Jonathan. They had their ups and downs, of course, but this was not through any fault of his. Nancy knew this and so deemed it unfair to speak about her husband negatively. He was her world, and she was his.

Nancy and Val made their way out of the hallway to collect their equipment and begin their rounds, changing and tidying rooms, meandering through the large corridors, taking the patients out and about, either in the TV and games room or accompanied to the garden for some fresh air. Nancy looked through the window and smiled, seeing her patients enjoying fleeting moments of happiness, one feeding birds, another reading on the memorial bench under the oak tree.

Val was a small, odd-looking woman who had recently divorced. Yet she always remained in high spirits, especially because it had been her choice to end the relationship. After realising that she had married out of duty rather than love, Val had decided to leave her husband. "That's what happens when you get yourself knocked up at 16," she would sometimes say. Val was bitterly lonely now that her husband was gone, and her two girls were grown up and married. Around 11 years previously, Val had lost her eldest daughter to a cardiac arrest. The girl was just 21 and had died in her sleep. It had happened very unexpectedly, and shocked everyone at Peacock Street, especially Nancy. It had been an awful time, and Val suffered a severe breakdown immediately after the death. She was understandably devastated and was off work for seven months. She did not leave her bed for five weeks, sometimes lying in a state of shock, silent and unresponsive, often intractable and angry, unable to speak to anyone who expressed sympathy, her disdain for the world directed towards each person who tried in vain to help her.

On one occasion when Nancy had visited, Val sat in her chair, but did not acknowledge Nancy when she walked in the door, ignoring her when Nancy said hello or turned on the kettle. Val sat staring at her living room wall and in the 40 minutes Nancy was there the only words she could muster were...

"Nothing is forever, and this is something I will forever remember."

"Nothing is forever."

"Nothing is forever."

"Nothing is forever."

As a result of her grief, Val had become increasingly ill and stopped eating. Nancy visited her every day, taking her cooked food, urging her to eat something, and supporting her through what could only be described as purgatory. Eventually, Val became healthier and stronger, and with the support of Nancy and Val's other devoted daughters, the anger dissipated and very gradually her happiness returned to small segments of her life, although she would often still cry on occasions, sometimes over nothing and sometimes at reminders of her lovely daughter, as small as a piece of jewellery, clothing, a TV show, or something as insignificant as a magazine she had liked when she was a teenager.

Around a year and a half after the passing of her daughter, a new girl, Amelia, had started work at Peacock Street. Amelia shared a striking resemblance to Val's late daughter; it was surprising to everyone who had met her when she was alive. The day Amelia started at the hospital, Val followed her around, chatting and at one point hugging her new colleague without warning. Thankfully, Amelia was understanding of the situation, and when Val eventually broke down in tears, she comforted her. Val was embarrassed that she had got carried away and apologised to her before they all left work. Most girls in Amelia's situation could have found it awkward, but Amelia handled the situation with kindness, so Nancy was pleased Val had a new friend.

Nancy would always know when Val was upset and was always there to give her the hug Val so desperately needed in those times of sadness. "I'm fine Nancy, thank you though love, honestly, I'm fine," Val would say, a little smile finally appearing at the side of her mouth. She was lonely, it was clear to Nancy. She would jokingly refer to herself as "used goods," but this was a front. It was transparent from her quietness and frequent overcompensation of happiness that Val was suffering more than she let on, and Nancy could see this.

In the dormitory, Val would often issue medication while Nancy would strip and remake beds. They would smile and laugh at the antics of the patients like Debbie Flint, a 20-stone 50-year-old who, as well as having the bad fortune of being institutionalised for severe depression, was also narcoleptic. This wrongly caused a few giggles among staff and patients due to her having to constantly wear a cycling helmet around the hard-tiled hospital just in case she fell asleep at any unfortunate moment. Many times, Nancy had found Debbie's huge body sprawled across the corridor like a jack-knifed lorry across a motorway, arms and legs in every manner of position. The nurses and patients would have to almost climb over her to get past. She would receive a stimulant and awaken from her slumber, unaware of what had happened moments before.

Debbie was not as you'd expect; aside from the burden's nature had inflicted on her and being the butt of many unfair jokes around the hospital from both patients and staff, she was quite self-aware of her affliction and how bizarre it was. Nancy had once asked Debbie when they were sitting together chatting in the TV room how she coped with her illnesses.

Debbie's reply was sombre. "Despite being in this place, I know what I am and who I am, I know that when you live with an affliction like this it's something you can't control, you just have to come to peace with it."

Nancy had thought long and hard about these words and what they meant. They had been the cause of many sleepless nights in her bed as she tossed and turned. At times she would watch her husband sleep, just to make sure he was ok, watching his chest rise and fall with every breath he took, so she knew he was alive and still with her, Debbie's profound words spiralling through her mind.

Fortunately, the depression Debbie suffered did not dampen her sense of humour. She was a natural comedienne, dry and cutting, but without malice. Her physical health issues were not the cause of her depression, which went deeper and darker than any insecurities that might naturally arise from her weight and narcolepsy. She would have nightmares while awake, and days of mutism. Her issues were born from a deeper place, a trauma the cause of which Nancy did not dare to speculate about.

Debbie's friend and dorm neighbour was another patient Nancy worked closely with at Peacock Street. Her name was Jayne Cob. A plain yet attractive woman with an unnaturally large nose, cropped blonde hair, and overly large blue eyes, she was what some people may describe as gawky. She would be found on many occasions wandering the corridors, entranced and detached from the outside world, sometimes reciting Shakespeare, Wordsworth and other literary greats. Although suffering from severe depression and acute schizophrenia, Jayne had a gift, a brilliant and complex mind comparable to few. She was a former English literature professor and scholar at King's College. She had been kind and gentle to everyone, especially her students, but somewhat naive.

Jaynes's story, like that of many of the other patients, was heart-wrenching and painful. Jayne had suffered a serious breakdown after one of her male students, a handsome individual named James, much younger than her, very charming and extremely ambitious, had manipulated his way into her life and eventually seduced her. After several months of what Jayne thought was a blissful romantic encounter, she was in love; she saw a future with this man and was at this point willing to risk everything for him, including her marriage and her job.

One evening, after two bottles of red wine and several whiskies, Jayne decided to confess her feelings and her desire to marry James, this man who had captured her heart, who consumed her every thought. Her only wish was to make a new life and a home with him, and finally find the happiness she had always wanted. All the while, she was unaware of the game that had been played out behind her back. This man she loved with all her heart, and to whom she had told great secrets and divulged important and confidential information, this man who while he lay in her bed would seek more and more information, also read through her notes and personal papers, stealing ideas, finding confidential material about the university. And if that wasn't enough, he also cheated on her with every girl on campus he flashed his soulless smile at. The whole horrible debacle concluded with Jayne being shunned and publicly humiliated at a prestigious university dinner, surrounded by her colleagues, students, parents, and local dignitaries, all watching in horror as these two lovers grappled and spilt the intricacies of their lives to everyone present. They hurled intimate insults, brazen clashes with such language and vindictiveness that many people had to cover their ears or leave.

Unsurprisingly, Jayne had already given him a first on his master's degree a month previously and lavished him with expensive gifts, just before the news had become public. This, again unsurprisingly, was far from the mark he deserved, had the affair not started. The situation left Jayne empty and inconsolably heartbroken, her fragile soul scorched forever.

Deeply mortified and having lost the will to live, Jayne attempted to take her own life with a cocktail of alcohol and some prescription drugs. This was not a call for help or an attempt to gain her former lover's attention; it was genuine and meant to be final. This is how she would find peace, an end to this torment. She had made her decision, but she had failed. Her efforts were thwarted by her sister-in-law Judy, the one person in the world who had felt sorry for her. Judy had found Jayne unconscious in a puddle of vomit and cheap vodka on her living room floor.

Once out of hospital, she waited until she knew everyone caring enough to check on her would be at work. This time, she meant to finish what she had started. She had a sense of calmness about her as she gathered the items she needed. Jayne thought that hanging herself from her banister would be more successful. But again, her plan was prevented by her sister-in-law, and the forgiving rope she had not tightened enough. Like the previous attempt, this was done with intent but lacked conviction. Jayne was released from the hospital, and for a while was able to stabilise herself, until her now ex-husband had refused her access to see her only daughter. The judge ruled that a woman who attempts suicide twice in two months is not a fit parent.

Jayne's final attempt at suicide was to jump from a high-rise car park, but her landing was cruelly cushioned by rubbish from the market below. She suffered minor injuries to her body, but because her head had hit a drainage pipe midway through her fall, her face was now severely disfigured on one side, the skin patched together like an old blanket, and her jaw now shockingly and tragically misshapen. With every turn of her head, the mirror reflected the woman she was before she met the boy, and the woman she was now. This third attempt meant that Jayne ultimately ended up in Peacock Street.

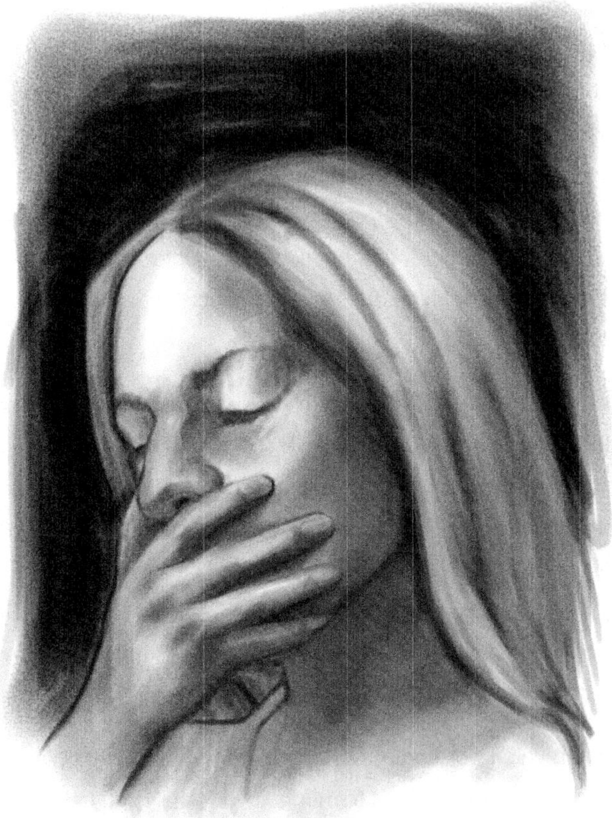

7 Chapter 7 – The Incident

7.1 June 1982

Nancy pulls into a space in the car park of the hospital and turns off the engine. She sits silently for a moment while her mind races with thoughts of how Henry might behave at home when he comes out of hospital, thoughts of Jonathan and her girls, how they would cope. They were all so excited about Henry coming home, but it had been so long. Her mind is thrown back to the day she had found Pebbles, the day of the incident, a day that changed their lives forever...

Nancy had returned home from work at lunchtime, as she sometimes did during the week. It was February, and a cold one at that. The morning had been long and monotonous, changing beds and administrating medicine, and all Nancy wanted was an hour to herself, an hour away from the gossip and the chaos of the hospital. Nancy had found herself becoming increasingly stressed recently and wanted some time alone to collect her thoughts. She had also remembered the cat needed to be fed, so there was no better excuse to use so that she could escape work for a much-needed break.

On arrival at her home, Nancy placed her bag on the kitchen table and proceeded to prepare the food for her beloved family cat, half a tin of cat meat, and a few biscuits, the same meal she always prepared. She called for Pebbles a few times, to no avail. "She'll be here when she smells the food," Nancy said under her breath, with mild apprehension. Pebbles was usually tucking into the food before Nancy could place it on the floor. Afterwards, she took out the bread and cheese and sat at her kitchen table, then positioned herself so she could look out the window and prepared her lunch.

Nancy sat at her dining table with her half-finished sandwich, her sketch book to her right and a Radio Times to her left. She doodled as she searched the listings of the magazine. She saw BBC 1 had 'Are You Being Served' at 7.30 and remembered how Jonathan always laughs at Mrs Slocombe. That would take them until 8ish, then perhaps they could all watch a film together, a family film. Maybe they could find a Disney tape—Emily loved Robin Hood with all the animals. Nancy, in recent weeks, had become extremely cautious about what her daughters were allowed to watch, being so young. The girls had watched One Flew Over the Cuckoo's Nest at a friend's house around four months before, and there had been a few sleepless nights afterwards, much to Nancy and Jonathan's annoyance.

As Nancy doodled, pencil in one hand, the second part of her sandwich in the other, she noticed another smaller book next to her fruit bowl at the other side of the table. It was small and tattered, and she recognised it as the one she had bought for Henry on his sixth birthday, a sketchbook with a soft brown suede cover, only slightly larger than her hand. She had not seen it in years, so it brought a smile to her face. She had always hoped that one of her children would have that artistic impulse that had always brought her so much pleasure throughout her life. She tapped her lips gently, considering what to do next. She took her hand from her face and placed it on the table. Tapping her fingers for a moment, pausing to consider whether to look inside. She carefully picked up the sketchbook, noting the blemishes on the skin, admiring the soft suede as she brushed it with her fingertips. It had obviously been very well used. Unable to contain her curiosity, although she better than anyone knows that an artist rarely wants their work exhibited to anyone, especially to their mum, Nancy opened the sketchbook. To her surprise, there were no pictures or sketches but words, poems and thoughts and more thoughts and more poems, pages filled with dark but beautiful literature. She stopped flicking through the pages and began to read something that had caught her eye, a poem with no title.

Today is hard, but yesterday it was fine,

How strange it is.

There is no reason nor rhyme,

The world is dark and cavernous. I feel,

These emotions that glut my heart,

These are the ones I must conceal.

A new day has come.

I no longer feel empty, sad, nor dumb,

I am alive.

Nancy read the words aloud, taking in each letter, each syllable. She was unsure if the poem was a sign of progress or regression. She felt slightly pleased that at least one of her children had the artistic flair she had hoped, even if it wasn't for her passion for painting and drawing. Still, the poems were mostly dark, depressive prose. She knew generally poets and writers use the pen to vent their frustrations with life, a cathartic measure used to suppress the demon emotions they have inside, and if anyone had those emotions, it was Henry. Nancy took some solace in this and the fact he had been, on the surface anyway, a happy and jovial 13-year-old for some time now and that teenagers, as she knew very well, could be dramatic and expressive, so she placed the book back where it had been moments before and continued to eat her sandwich. She would have a talk with Henry just to see if all was ok later that evening. Once Nancy finished her sandwich, she began to get increasingly worried about the family pet, so she decided to make the effort to look for her cat. "Pebbles, here darling, where are you?". Nothing. So, she stood and started to search the house. She looked everywhere, in all her usual hiding places, behind the sofa, under the bed, under the old blanket in the utility room, in the shed, all to no avail. She looked under hedges in both the front and back garden. Although slightly worried, she convinced herself that Pebbles would be back when she was hungry and not to worry.

On her way back into the house, she noticed a head poking over her next-door neighbours' fence. The house next door was larger than Nancy's and Jonathan's, a Tudor style with a beautiful orchard in the garden, the largest on the street.

"Hello, Mrs Ferriman, how are you today?" Nancy says as she sees a flash of red cur

Mrs Ferriman, the family's elderly neighbour, would often look after the girls and occasionally Henry after school. She was incredibly sweet and adored all of Nancy's children, especially Henry. She had doted on him from a young age, much like Nancy had. She said that he reminded her of her son, David, whom she had lost during the Second World War. David was a war hero, and Mrs Ferriman would often recount the story of how he saved his own battalion, or what was left of them when they had been surrounded by enemy soldiers. The only gunshot wounds sustained that heroic day were two shots to David's shoulder, after which he had developed a trauma-related infection and died of a blood clot two weeks later in a military hospital in France. Mrs Ferriman had never had the opportunity to say goodbye to her only son, and she missed him dearly. Henry was a way she could get back some semblance of those years she had missed with her own son.

Nancy had stopped taking the children around, because Mrs Ferriman had started saying quite openly that she often spoke to her deceased son and that he would visit her most nights. Nancy did not feel this was a very healthy thing for her young children to hear. It also brought up some unnerving memories of her own grandmother, talking to ghosts and spirits, and her unusual behaviour in her family house. But this day, Mrs Ferriman seemed unusually normal as she clipped her roses.

Mrs Ferriman looked over at Nancy, smiled, and waved. "How are you dear?" she loudly said so that Nancy could clearly hear, then proceeded to walk towards her neighbour at the edge of her short driveway. "I gather there's some sort of teacher training day today, Nancy? Is that right? Seems odd on a Wednesday, but what do I know?"

To Nancy´s knowledge, there most certainly was not a teacher training day, because she had dropped her children at school that very morning and she could see all the students arrive in uniform. "I don't think so, Jane, I dropped the kids off this morning, 8.30 am as per usual, why do you ask?"

Now Mrs Ferriman was the one who looked confused. "Well, I saw Henry not an hour ago, on the drive, right where you're stood now, actually. He was heading to the park with a plastic bag in his hand. I asked why he wasn't at school today and he said it was a teacher training day."

Nancy´s demeanour immediately changed as she tried to understand why Henry wasn't at school. A look of panic appeared on her face. "I have to go, Jane, thank you for letting me know." Nancy proceeded to run towards the park, leaving a concerned Mrs Ferriman in her wake, her mind still racing. She sensed something was badly wrong, the feeling slowly consuming her. She ran until she was out of breath, then continued until she almost fainted, passing her neighbours' houses one by one, not able to stop and respond to the "Hello," "How are you?" and "Are you ok?" that she heard on her way. The final path to the park was long, you could not drive there so she trudged through the mud, her uniform and shoes caked in more and more filth with every step. It had been a particularly wet morning and a mist had settled on the field on which the park was built. Nancy proceeded to search for her son, the dense fog making the task considerably harder. Nancy looked in the children's playground and then near the football pitches, then around the village hall, which was situated on the opposite side of the field near the main entrance.

After 25 minutes of searching and calling for her son, all to no avail, she had no choice but to give up. After taking a moment to think, Nancy had now calmed down slightly. She told herself she would discipline Henry for his truancy when he arrived home later, but for now, she had to get back to work. Nancy was now both late for work and covered in mud, but she knew Andrea would cover for her. She would call as soon as she got home and explain that she would happily work late if needed. She knew Nurse McKinnock would kick up a fuss, but at this point, walking through a cold field covered in mud, she did not care.

As Nancy left the field through the stile, finally looking down and seeing how filthy she really was, she noticed something poking out of the hedge on the other side of the fence to her left. Whatever it was, it was covered in grass and leaves. It had caught her eye because it was the brown hessian grocery bag she used for her shopping. The bag was bulging, and she was intrigued. Nancy managed to squeeze through a gap in the far side of the fence and walked over to the now swampy grassland towards the bag about 20 metres from where it had first caught her eye. When Nancy got there, she brushed aside the twigs and grass and picked up the bag and looked inside, there curled up in the bottom, neck broken, mangled and covered in blood, was Pebbles, petrified and wet, a face of horror frozen in time.

Nancy dropped the bag, and it fell onto the wet grass. She took a step back. The shock of what she had seen rendered her speechless. For a moment, she couldn't bring herself to look again. Nancy stood with her eyes closed, hands trembling by her side. When she finally looked down, Pebble's head was at her feet, poking out of the bag, like a stuffed mount that has fallen from a wall. Suddenly her sadness dissipated, and anger started to set in, rage at her son, at what he'd done, not only to her but the rest of their family. How selfish to take Pebble from them, the cat the girls adored, the cat she thought he adored. Nancy thought back to all the times he had upset the family, how he had hurt Jonathan, the names he would call him, and how she would try to defend her son, to the detriment of her relationship with the only man she had ever loved, and the man she adored, his beautiful soul being picked at and worn with every one of Henry's words.

Nancy gently picked Pebbles up and placed her head back in the bag, drops of blood dripping steadily from her tiny mouth. This was the last straw; something had to be done. Two days later, Henry was committed to Broadway Boy's Psychiatric Facility.

8 Chapter 8 – The Lunchroom

8.1 March 1984 – Present day

Nancy is sitting at lunch, only a few bites of her sandwich left, and a sip of tea. She is sketching in her book, the one she keeps at work, away from prying eyes. It was a secret from everyone; no one had ever seen what was inside. As much as she loved drawing and painting her family and friends, or sketching a squirrel eating nuts, or a majestic old oak tree, or an old man sitting on a bench in the woods, it was at work that she could really see all the deepest emotions humans can express, both candid and raw. Sadness, joy, grief, and despair, all fully characterised in the patients, and occasionally in her colleagues' faces. Nancy had by this time sketched many, if not most, of her patients and a few colleagues, sometimes while sitting on her break, or from memory while she sat on her bed in the overnight room, or occasionally in the garden under the large oak tree from which she could see the herb garden. She had a gift for remembering details—an expanding wrinkle on the forehead of a colleague, a unique expression of one of her subjects, or even the way a blanket draped, then falls over the shoulders of one or other of her patients. Her drawings are generally, as one might assume, based on the environment from which she draws her inspiration, dark and morose, but they are catharsis in an otherwise depressing place.

"Nancy! Are you going to do any work today, or is your job to perpetually chat to the nurses?" Miss Kinnock shouts, noticing Nancy looking a bit too comfortable for someone who should be returning to work imminently.

"No, Miss Kinnock," Nancy coyly replies to her boss's quite flippant remark, careful not to make eye contact with her intimidating boss. The clock hits 12:30, and as if a bell had rung in the playground, patients and nurses begin to get up and shuffle around the tables, leaving the large dining room and going in all different directions, some heading to the garden, some to therapy, some to the television room where a young man volunteers to teach music to patients. "That hippy is back," Val had said, looking at the young man who led the music group. Tom had just slightly longer hair than the norm, but in Val's opinion, this was enough to qualify him as a hippy.

The old Georgian building that houses the hospital causes a stir of echoes from the voices and noises of the dining room that rings through Nancy's ears like an orchestra. Every morning, she is taken back to her school days. It reminds her of her friends sitting around in their large school hall, playing playful pranks on their peers and teachers. Happy times, she thinks to herself, as the moment of nostalgia causes her to force a reticent smile. Old Kinnock looks over sharply, and Nancy closes her sketch book and finally looks at her boss. She notices McKinnock's head is like one of the hawks in her garden, scanning for its next mouse to swoop in on.

Val very fervently stands up and with a wry smile on her face, tells the remaining nurses, "The quicker we get working, the quicker I get home to my boyfriend Sean Connery." The nurses around the table begin to stand and gather their possessions and clipboards.

"Mr Bond and I actually have plans tonight, so you'll have to find another man, Valerie," Nancy remarks playfully as they smile at each other. A few nurses giggle and disperse to their relevant jobs and posts. Nancy and Val link arms.

"You have your Mr Bond, my girl, let me have mine," Val whispers back with a wink and a chuckle.

Mrs McKinnock, still on the lookout for wayward behaviour, barks over to Val and Nancy. "Val, you're on change over duty today. Take Nancy as well." She does not even look over in their general direction or change facial expression. A look of melancholy appears on Val's face. Today Nancy and Val are changing the rooms of the recently deceased.

9 Chapter 9 – The Funeral

9.1 March 1984 – Present day

To end one's life in Peacock Street Hospital is a sad end. You are buried in the grounds and very often with only a few nurses in attendance. If you're lucky, one or two members of your immediate family will also attend, although the sad truth is that a lot of the visitors are generally there only to collect the remaining belongings, in case anything of any value had passed under the radar. This was the exact situation Nancy was witnessing from the third-floor room she was clearing and changing with Val.

Margaret Dipple, a middle-aged woman committed by her father as a young girl due to her moderate learning disabilities, was being slowly lowered to her resting place only 100 yards from the building. The six nurses who treated her and her twin sister were the only attendees, all arched around the hole where Margaret finally lay. The women all sobbed, not only at the death of Margaret, but at the wasted life of a kind and gentle woman, by the end of her life intelligent and witty, who was subjected to undeserved cruelty and rejection.

Margaret was, on any given day, the life and soul of Peacock Street, holding court whenever there were visitors, and ever the ideal ambassador for the institution. Margaret was the consummate romantic and believed, despite her circumstances, that she would meet her prince charming, and he would finally take her to faraway lands where they would dance under the moonlight. This ideal was a product of too many movies and books she had watched and read throughout her life at the institution, but this fiction and imagination was, even though she was bright enough to realise the limited possibilities of this, of little relevance to her.

"What do people have if they don't have dreams, especially here, especially in a place like this. If I can bring a little bit of happiness to others and myself, then I will," Margaret would say. Her gregarious nature was a wonder to all who met her. Small glimmers of light in people are needed; it is infectious, and it is necessary for a happy life, Nancy thought after hearing this. Margaret radiated this with every bone in her body.

Margaret would often dance in and around the rooms, spreading much-needed joy and love to a generally dismal and depressing place. Frequently, patients and occasionally staff would join her dancing to whatever song the radio or vinyl that day had to offer.

Margaret had finally suffered a fatal stroke, after a lifetime of heart complications, but still, until her last moments on this Earth, she believed her prince would finally come.

Though the day could not be more soulless, the clouds dark and dramatic are seemingly conscious of the situation Nancy is witnessing. The rain falls lightly on the window as Nancy is transfixed on the tragic scene below. Margaret's sister reaches into her handbag and gently pulls out an old book. She effortlessly drops it into the grave. Unsure of the relevance, Nancy's mind begins to wander. She concludes that this is perhaps Margaret and her sister's childhood book, maybe one their mother would read to them as they fell asleep at night. Nancy feels a tightening in her throat. She tries to stop it, but the tears come anyway. They slowly roll down Nancy's face and fall to the windowsill below. As the nurses start to return to the building, the caretakers begin to fill the hole with little sympathy or decorum. Margaret's sister wipes away her last tear with her white handkerchief, then turns and walks to her car.

"Goodbye sweet angel, I will never forget you," Nancy whispers to Margaret as this beautiful woman dances through her thoughts, happy and content, lovingly embraced in the arms of her prince charming.

"What's going on out there?" Val says, as if this were a daily occurrence. "Poor old Margaret." Nancy quickly follows, pulling herself together, snapping out of her solemn trance, realising what was going on and where she is.

"It makes me so very sad when funerals happen, Val," Nancy confesses, her voice breaking slightly in her repeated attempts not to cry. "I feel like we should make more of an effort with the patients here after they pass on, perhaps celebrate their life rather than a few words and a hole in the ground."

Val lifts her head and frowns at Nancy from over her crooked glasses. Nancy hates this look from Val; she can predict the condescending comment that will inevitably fall from Val's lips. "Now Nancy, don't be getting yourself into trouble with your silly ideas and hassling old McKinnock again, you remember what happened the last time!" Nancy did remember; she'd had an idea about taking the patients for days out to the park and seaside. After proposing her idea in the dinner hall in front of the staff and patients, Miss McKinnock had called her a 'naive imbecile' and stood up with such fury that her dinner flew off the table where she had quietly been eating and ended up landing the lap of one of the patients. The man, a patient named Bryson Collins (or as the staff called him, 'The Cleaning Man') had begun to cry due to the commotion and then many of the other patients had followed. It was, as Val and Nancy remembered, a tough afternoon.

Bryson Collins was always fastidiously immaculate in every way. Not a speck of dust in his room. He dressed every day like an English gentleman, jacket and tie, polished black shoes, and pin with the royal crest. An extremely charismatic gentleman afflicted with severe OCD and depression, he had been admitted after he was found attempting to groom a young man with whom he had become obsessed.

Bryson had been admitted to Peacock Street Hospital around the time Nancy had started. Because of this, they had built a silent bond, both being the newcomers. They talked often and in depth about all sorts of things. He was prone to severe depression, and so she enjoyed his happy days more. The wittiest man she had ever met, she always said, sometimes to the point of being acerbic. He was worldly, and she adored hearing over and over about his adventures. She had been informed by Bryson that the boy he had been accused of grooming had flirted and lied to him about his age, and he had been foolish enough to fall for his youthful charm. When the young man's father had found out about the relationship the authorities were alerted and Bryson was labelled a predator. Because of his age, he was placed in the care of the nurses at Peacock Street Hospital.

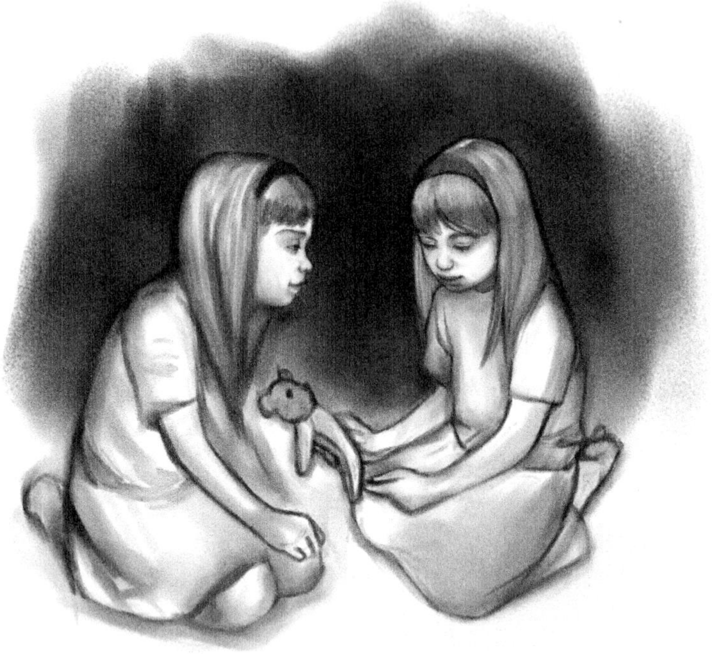

10 Chapter 10 – The Miracle

10.1 October 1976

For the first six months of Henry's life, Nancy did not let him out of her sight. He was constantly within her arm's reach; she was with him always. But gradually over the following years, this started to decrease, and eventually Jonathan got his wife back. He knew he would eventually, so he gave Nancy the time she needed to adapt. The time she craved with Henry.

Henry, from a young age, did not take to his father like he did his mother. Although all the while Jonathan continued to be as loving and attentive as a father could be, he could not compete with Nancy. She doted on him. If Henry wanted something, he ultimately would get it. Toys, games, clothes, anything he desired. Nancy spoilt him in every way.

Unfortunately, due to the relationship Henry had developed with his mother, his reliance on her was constant and tiring. He was increasingly irritated when she was not around; if he could not see her, he was a meerkat scouting where she might be. He would have fits of jealous rage if she interacted with others, including Jonathan, and especially other children. Nancy blamed herself for this, and her guilt hit hard when Henry acted up. When Henry was seven, after trying all the calming techniques available, the local GP recommended a drug used for children with hyperactive disorders to see if it would calm Henry down. Desperate and exhausted, the couple reluctantly bought the drug and administered the dosage, still sceptical, but hopeful for the medication's success. Over the following weeks, Nancy would add this to his food every day, morning, and night, but to the couple's dismay, there was no change. Henry's issues were consistent, his rage, his need for his mother—they all persisted despite the medication.

About a week before Henry's eighth birthday, the week they had finally decided to stop giving him his medication and try an alternative method, a miracle occurred.

On a drizzly cold October morning, Nancy and Jonathan were having breakfast at their pine dining table. It was a Saturday, so Jonathan was not working. The rain trickled down their patio doors, the rhythmic sound of drops tapping away on the windowsill outside. Nancy had made Jonathan eggs and toast while he read the morning paper, periodically sipping from his coffee cup, glasses perched on the end of his nose. Henry had been left to sleep after a particularly uneasy evening, after which the couple had chatted about their plans for the weekend. They planned on taking Henry out to the park, to try and get him to interact with his father and maybe some other children—a technique they had tried numerous times without success. They discussed how the Monday after the weekend would be his last dose of the medication, and what their next step would be. As Nancy poured herself her first cup of tea of the morning, she noticed the door open slightly and a little body sneak in.

"Henry, is that you darling? I have your breakfast here." He was standing just inside the doorway, looking around the kitchen. Henry was small for his age. He looked six at most in this moment, tiny belly protruding from his pyjamas. His eyes were sleepy and the back of his wavy auburn hair, like his father's, was sticking up. He rubbed his eyes and yawned.

"Hello, my little man," Jonathan said, looking over his spectacles. His tone was almost desperate for a reaction, a longing for something back from his son. There was a moment of stillness as Henry looked at his father, then walked slowly to the table where Jonathan was sitting, arms outstretched. Henry climbed onto his father's lap, settled in, not saying a word; he breathed softly as he rested his head on his father's dressing-gown-covered chest. Nancy and Jonathan looked at each other. They were dumbstruck but elated. Nancy started to cry at the sight of this colossal moment, but she was beaten by her husband, who was overcome with the paternal acceptance he had craved for so long. He held his son close, kissing him on the forehead as if to confirm the bond. Henry closed his eyes and drifted back to sleep.

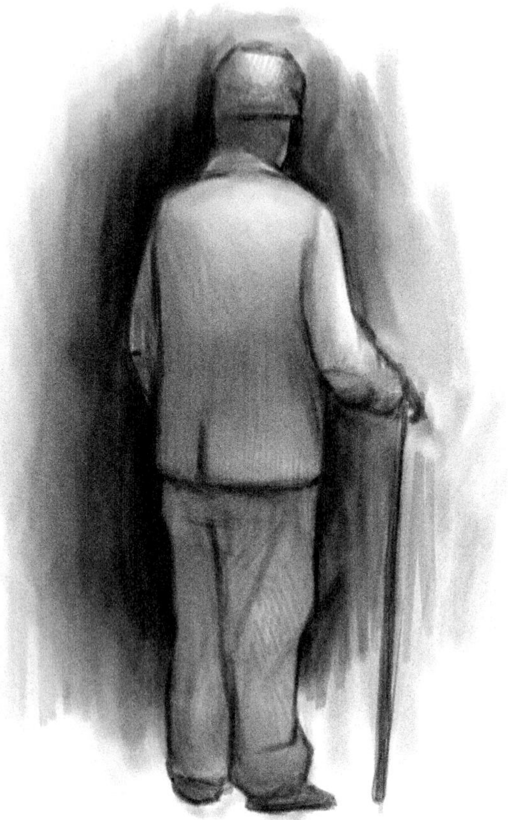

11 Chapter 11 – The TV Room

11.1 March 1984 – Present day

Dinnertime comes around quickly, and Nancy and Val have made good time on the rooms they have been changing. Margaret's funeral has made Nancy anxious, and she can't seem to shake it. Nancy feels out of sorts, slightly removed from herself. She rests for a second on the freshly made bed.

"Good job today, Nancy. The old battle axe will be pleased," Val says, sensing something is wrong. Of course, she is referring to their boss, the delightful Nurse McKinnock. Val chuckles to herself as she loads the dirty linen from their last room into the large basket trolley and heads back towards the main corridor, Nancy following closely behind.

The rain has stopped, but the day is still dull. The hospital is gloomy and hollow; it has not been re-decorated in at least 20 years, Nancy estimates as she walks slowly through the halls. The walls are cold and bare apart from the odd faded watercolour hanging up in the long hallways. Brass beds are lined up in rows for patients on either side of two long rooms at the back of the hospital, one male, one female, a narrow walkway down the middle for entry to each bed space. The ceilings are high and cavernous, so every unsavoury and unnecessary sound is heard by all.

"Nancy, can you check on the TV room please, just to make sure everyone is behaving… if you're not too busy that is, although you do not look it currently, my dear!" Nancy hears Mrs McKinnock bellow from the bottom of the corridor. "Remember, Nancy, you are not special, and you are not unique. You are the same as everyone else. Get on with your job." Nancy does not respond but rolls her eyes at the comment, after making sure no one sees. Mrs McKinnock is chatting with two other nurses who are laughing at the tirade they have just witnessed. Nancy obliges, even though officially her afternoon break has already started. Best not to poke the beast, she thought, on the cusp of a witty comeback.

As Nancy enters the lounge, the television is deafening. Two patients watch intently as Nancy turns down the volume slightly, but they are unfazed by the change, remaining hypnotised by what they are watching. One is drooling slightly, so Nancy gently wipes her face before moving on. The lounge is bustling, and the room has a life of its own; distorted voices echo around the room, disguised underneath the unnecessary high volume of the television.

The old drawing room is now the TV and games lounge. It is, in Nancy's opinion, the nicest room in the hospital. A beautiful ornate Victorian fireplace is the centre piece; it is where patients and nurses gather in the cold winter months. The traditional coving on all cross-sections of the wall completes the traditional exquisiteness of this former drawing-room. Nancy looks around all four corners to ensure everything is okay.

Mary Evans is playing chess with Barry Thompkins, both middle-aged and widowed far too early by the war. Mary, a manic depressive, and Barry, severely bipolar, are both self-committed; they are the only two in the whole hospital like this, and on the mild end of the scale for patients within Peacock Street. They have both improved in leaps and bounds since coming in, Barry, five, and Mary six months ago. They will, Nancy hopes, for their own sake, be leaving soon.

"I hope you two keep in touch when you leave," Nancy says, her undertone suggesting that perhaps there could be slightly more to the relationship than just a friendship, an obvious romance that has enchanted both patients and nurses for months. Nancy hopes there is. "It could be the very thing they need," she thinks, two lonely people battling through this cruel life, both with demons they fight back every day. Maybe the solution is not Peacock Street Hospital, Nancy thought. Maybe the drugs and the endless counselling sessions aren't the remedy, and love is. Maybe it's that simple.

Barry and Mary look at each other slightly abashed. "I can't imagine Mary could last a day without me now," he says, amusingly nonchalant, still playing his turn in the game of chess they were so close to finishing. A cheeky wink over at Nancy, confirming the joke.

"Ha!" Mary responds sharply, "This old sod will be round at my kitchen table every day I should think, he's fallen for my good looks and wit… and my cooking, obviously". Barry and Nancy laugh.

"I'm sure he has, Mary, who wouldn't?" Nancy replies as she spots Barry's tender smile directing itself at Mary. "Love is a great healer," Nancy says quietly to herself as she walks away, leaving Barry to let Mary win for the hundredth time.

Nancy continues her rounds of the TV room, chatting, while checking all patients are ok. She is happy that all is well. She then stops, hearing a familiar voice, and looks around the room.

"Who's that?" She recognises the voice coming from the television. She knows this voice and she knows this programme. A proud smile spreads on her face, and she turns to see a group of patients watching a rerun of the programme her husband had worked on for so many years. The familiarity of the characters she recognises, and she walks over, still revelling in that feeling of pride. "Hang on a second," Nancy mumbles to herself. She knows the programme, but she can't work out if it's a new episode or a very old one. She is taken aback. She's never seen this episode before. The programme is the same, but the people are different.

"What programme is this?" she asks Jayne Cobb. Jayne is sitting in her usual armchair, legs crossed and dour, for a change not smoking or reading or both.

"That awful comedy the BBC's managed to drag on all these years, Jesus! The plot is deplorable, and the writing… well! I never, I could… I could do a better job on the loo, I'm sure, my fucking ten-year-old daughter could write something funnier, it used to be remotely entertaining and funny but now… absolute rubbish!" This causes a few laughs from the other patients, who seem to be enjoying it despite the scathing review. Nancy decides to ignore Jayne's comments; she is a professional and Jayne does not know her husband's connection to the programme. Nancy tells the patients as little as possible about her home life, just the same as most of the nurses. It's standard procedure and common sense; some of the younger, newer nurses had been caught out by divulging too much to patients about their personal lives. One of the girls, Shona, was called an 'Irish slut' after telling a patient about a breakup with her boyfriend, and how she had found someone new and was happy with her new partner. Many of the patients could be cruel, possessing a fundamental lack of empathy due to their illnesses and the medications they had to take.

Nancy stands for a while trying to make sense of the episode. "When did this air? Why haven't I seen it?" she ponders to herself for a while. Minutes pass like seconds until finally, Miss McKinnock pokes her head around the door.

"Sister Blake, I believe you should be in the laundry presently, not watching this rubbish." Nancy is abruptly woken from her second daydream of the day.

"Yes Miss McKinnock, I was just… just going."

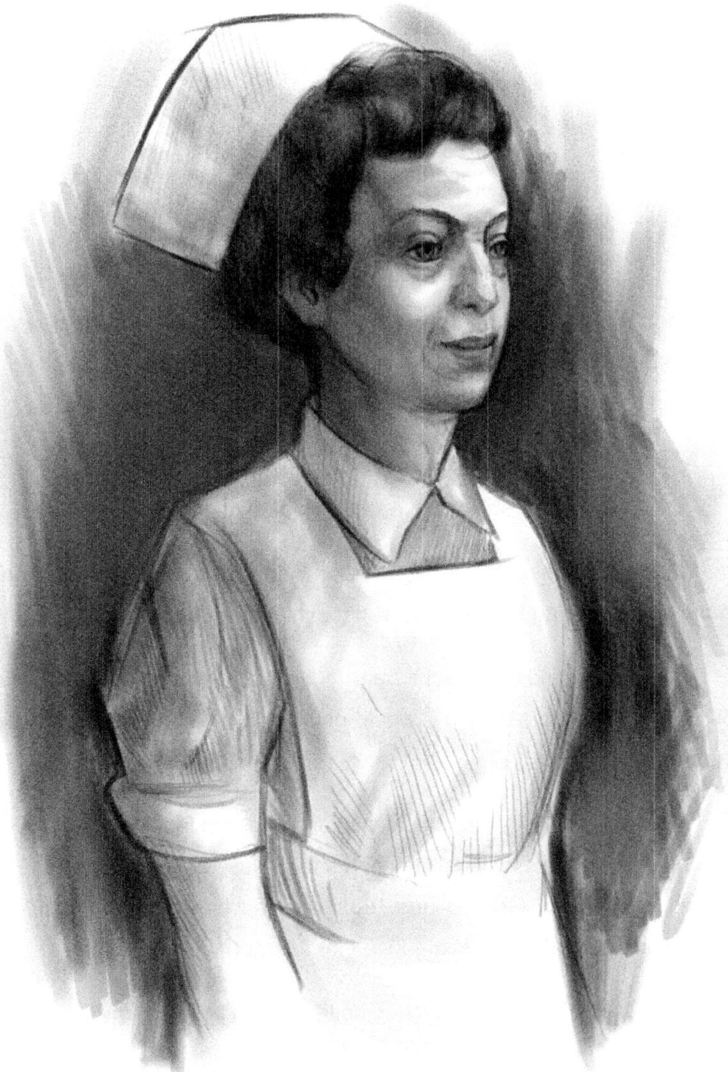

12 Chapter 12 – The Homecoming

12.1 July 1982

"Do we have to go to school today, Mum? Can we stay at home, please! Just today! I'll be really good, and I'll do all my homework!" Nancy looked at her daughter with her 'you know better than to ask this question' eyes.

"No, Emily, you know you can't take days off school, willy nilly. It doesn't work like that. Henry will still be here when you get back from school and your father and I won't be home till around two, anyway." Sarah, who knew better than to push her luck, was already in the car ready for her trip to school.

"Ok, I suppose," Emily said, easily defeated and grinning cheekily.

"Can we at least get ice cream when Henry gets home, Mum? Please?" she pleaded, knowing her mum's a soft touch in these situations.

"Yes, Emily, now put your belt on and chat with your sister," Nancy replied, exasperated, knowing it would give her a moment of peace from her daughter.

In the car, Emily talked about what fun things the family could do over the weekend with Henry, how she'll tell him she's missed him and how sad she'd been while he'd been away so long. "First, we'll have a barbeque, then a water fight, then play Scrabble…" she paused for thought.

"No! Cards… Henry likes cards better, doesn't he Mummy?"

"Yes, cards, it's the best game for Henry. What else can we do, Sarah?" Sarah was more reserved. She stared out the window, smiling occasionally at Emily's ambitious plans for Henry and the family.

"Then we'll go to the zoo, then the seaside, then we can take a boat up the river like we did that time with Daddy, then... Hmmm, we could go on holiday. Yes, Henry will like that, won't he, Mummy?" Emily continued relentlessly, but Nancy was not listening; she was in a world of her own. As she dropped the girls at school, she forgot to give them their lunches, still unable to concentrate on her thoughts. Emily was still giddy and talkative even as she exited the car. Nancy was apprehensive about her son's homecoming, and she could not seem to shake it.

The road leading up to Broadway Hospital was long. Nancy meandered through the one-and-a-half-mile arch of London Plaines. She leaned forward and looked up through her windscreen to get a better view of the roof of the trees on either side of her. She saw them meeting in the middle, creating a silhouette of branches, the sunlight every few seconds breaking through and dazzling her. For a moment, she forgot her doubts and worries, the fears dissipated, and she saw trips away with her family. A life less complicated, a moment where she hadn't lost those last nine months of her life, months worrying whether she'd ever see her son again, sleepless nights, the calls from the hospital, the strain it had taken on her family is all at once gone, until she pulled up at the hospital and the reality had slowly crept back. "Come on, Nancy, your son's coming home today," she smiled at herself reassuringly in her rear-view mirror, and pictured her family on the beach, her husband sat on a deck chair next to her with Emily on his lap, while Henry and Sarah played in the sea.

The hospital was modern but depressing, a brutalist ensemble of grey and white building materials. Nancy parked her car and walked to the entrance, where she was buzzed into the reception. The interior was equally as depressing, magnolia walls and plastic plants throughout. The overpowering smell of cleaning products started to make Nancy's eyes water and caused her to gag slightly.

"How is Henry today?" Nancy asked one of the nurses on his corridor.

"Oh, he's fine, he's had his lunch and was reading the last time I saw him." The nurse could see Nancy's anxiety and worried expression. "From what he said, he's looking forward to going home and sleeping in his own bed," the nurse said reassuringly, and Nancy managed to break a nervous smile, a sigh of relief escaped her lips as she responds, her voice breaking slightly.

"Thank you so much and thank you for taking care of him" she managed to say.

"It's no problem. He's a good boy" the nurse said empathetically, as she exited the corridor into another room.

Waiting in his bedroom, perched on the edge of the bed and facing the door was Henry, holding his notebook, his bags by his side, all packed and ready to leave. He was dressed in the new clothes Nancy had bought him and given to him on her last visit there. His head was bent, staring at his feet, like a daydreaming infant sitting on a stool that's too tall for them. Nancy watched him for a moment. The stillness could be endless. He did not flinch; without his slow breathing rhythm, the room could have been a photograph or a painting, something you'd see in an exhibition, with a title something like 'Within the Sadness of a Moment' or similar. Finally, Henry noticed his mum at the door and slowly lifted his head. A smile appeared on his face, a smile that is neither happy nor sad, but Nancy was pleased, nonetheless. It took all the muscles in her body to stop herself crying. Henry then stood up and picked his bag up off the floor.

"Shall we go home, Mum?" he said as he gave her a soft smile.

On the drive home, Henry was quiet. The silence was mildly uncomfortable, but Nancy was thrilled to have a semblance of the son she once knew sitting next to her, nonetheless. Henry did nothing for a while but stare out the window, answering questions only when asked, and occasionally changing the radio station. Nancy looked over from time to time and wondered what he was thinking. He was neither animated at leaving the hospital nor disappointed. She dismissed it, and the hour-long drive home was as pleasant as Nancy could hope for. She had her son, and for the first time in what felt like forever, she began to feel her stomach unwind and the weight of the world drop from her shoulders.

Nancy and Henry pulled into the drive where the family congregation was waiting. Dad, the two girls, and Jonathan's parents. Henry was first out of the car, and both girls rushed to greet him, arms out in anticipation. Henry reacted by throwing his arms around them both and hugging them tightly. It was the first real smile anyone had seen from him for a very long time. He loved his sisters more than anything, and it was more than evident in their embrace.

"We missed you Henry," said Sarah, eyes closed, both sisters' heads resting on each of Henry's shoulders.

"We really, really missed you. I hope you're better now," Emily retorted, not to be outdone by her elder sister. Henry eventually pulled away and hugged his grandparents, Jeanie and Dave, both well into their 70s and not fully aware of the circumstances surrounding Henry's long absence. They knew he had been ill, but the details were not disclosed. Finally, Henry hugged Jonathan, his head rested on his dad's right shoulder, face down, with Jonathan's hand gently resting on the back of his son's head.

"I missed you, Dad," Henry said, voice slightly muffled over the top of his dad's shirt.

"It's good to have you home, son, so very good." Both men calling a silent truce to their turbulent relationship.

"Well, I'm sure Henry is starving. Have you eaten since lunch, dear?" Jeanie asked her visibly emotional grandson, trying to get things back to normal as quickly as possible.

"No Gran, I am actually pretty hungry you know. I'm sure you've made your famous trifle for dessert," Henry kindly responded, smiling at his grandmother's efforts as well as quietly appreciating the focus being taken off him slightly. The whole family all retreated inside for dinner, happily chatting with each other.

Nancy was last in. She was happy, but something loomed inside her, a fear she could not explain or reason away. She dismissed it as nerves. She was aware of her constant nervousness, prone to worrying about everything. She put it down to the anxiety of change and the precarious nature of Henry's situation. Nancy looked out across the street, then up at the pink cloudy sky. She saw the usually magenta blossom blowing in the wind, but against the pink hazy sky it looked red, a deep red she had never seen before. "That's unusual," she said quietly to herself, and closed her door behind her.

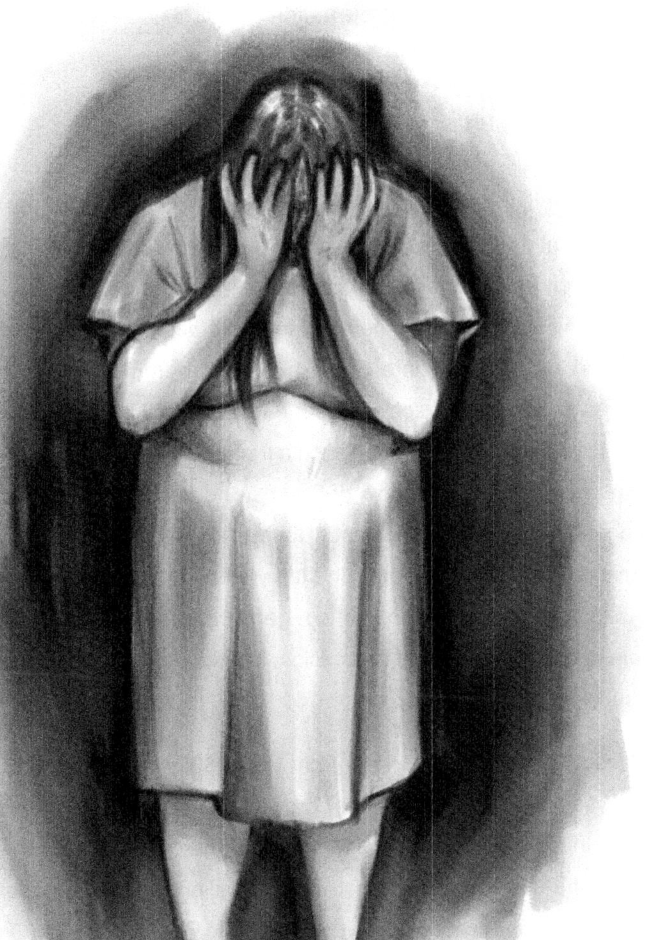

13 Chapter 13 - The Boys on the beach

13.1 March 1984 – Present day

"Hello Bryson, my dear. How are you today? I noticed that you've been a bit quiet recently. I just wanted to make sure you were ok, you know I'm a worrier," Nancy says, concerned. Bryson was always quiet, but after a morning spent cleaning up after the residents, Nancy had decided to look in on him now that she had five minutes spare. She liked to do this from time to time to ensure he was okay. He wasn't a social person and generally kept to himself most of the time. Bryson had been through such a traumatic time in his life; he had been bullied and victimised, a shadow of the man he used to be, his sunken eyes reflecting the anguish of his past. Nancy felt a deep connection to him, something she could not fathom. She felt very comfortable around him, unlike many of the other patients. Bryson is a gentle man who, through the sadness apparent in his ever-sorrowful expression, is kind and warm to all the people in the hospital, especially Nancy.

Nancy looks over at Bryson from her position at the edge of the living room. Bryson is sitting in his usual brown, well-worn leather armchair. This armchair, unlike the others, is positioned outward from the room, alone, and left apart from the other armchairs that are all positioned around the television or the fireplace. A book is open on Bryson's lap, The Picture of Dorian Gray. Nancy notices from the front cover that has flicked up that Bryson is not reading it. He is staring at a painting on the wall of the room. The painting depicts two young boys in their late teens, sitting on a large rock on the edge of a beach, with a dazzling honeycomb sun shining on the horizon and with ocean water that is so perfectly blue it beckons you in. Both boys seem to be in a conversation, and one has a rock in his hand. The boy on the right has blonde hair and is in a midmotion throw, while the boy on the left has slightly darker hair. He is watching his topless friend in admiration. The boy on the left, who is the subject of this adulation, is flexing his immutable muscles, his arm drawn back, in preparation for throwing a rock into the azure and turquoise ocean. The sand between the rocks is golden brown, with only the boys' footprints and a small red crab escaping through a gap towards the ocean.

Bryson sits motionless, staring longingly at the painting. Only the middle and index fingers of his right hand gently touch his bottom lip, and his left hand keeps his page.

"What a beautiful painting," Nancy remarks as she walks the length of the room towards him. She, too, is now captivated by the two immortal boys dwelling on that rock on the beautiful beach. Bryson remains silent as Nancy stops beside him. She rests her hand on his shoulder, and he returns to the room and finally acknowledges Nancy.

"Hello, my dear, yes, sorry, I'm fine thank you. I just put up one of my old paintings in here, I hope you don't mind. Nurse Kinnock said it was fine to do so. I had it in my room but there was no space to hang it, unfortunately. I only found it the other day, thought it would brighten up the place, what do you think?" Nancy looks at Bryson, slightly perplexed, and then back at the painting.

"Did you paint this, you sneaky thing?" Nancy comments with a titter and an unintentional surprised tone, "Sorry, I mean to say it's extraordinary, it's absolutely breath-taking, I can't praise it enough, the colours, it's so bright and intense but serene at the same time. I just didn't know you could paint, Bryson, my apologies." Nancy, now slightly embarrassed, begins to retreat from where she is standing.

"Wait, my dear," Bryson says, softly holding out his hand to her, a wry smile emerging on his face, while he still stares at the painting. "You're right, Nancy, I can't paint, never have. Unfortunately, I don't have an artistic bone in my body to be truthful. This was painted by someone I knew a long time ago, someone very special to me." Nancy takes Bryson's outstretched hand and pulls up a stool. They sit for a moment, both analysing this painting that was the subject of their conversation. Nancy knows she should not pry, but she cannot help but wonder who this mystery artist could be. She is aware of Bryson's past and how it had triggered many episodes in his time at the hospital, but she cannot help herself.

"Bryson, do you mind... umm... if I ask you who painted this? It's so beautiful. I understand if you don't want to tell me, that's completely fine of course, I wouldn't want to overstep the mark".

Bryson takes his left hand off his overturned book and places it on top of Nancy's. He looks at her and smiles. "Can I tell you a story, Nancy? It's my story of the painting, if you'd like to hear it of course." Nancy smiles and squeezes his fingers. From the look on his face, she can tell this story is going to be special.

"Yes, please, dear. I would absolutely love to hear your story." She replies with eagerness.

13.2 July 1931

"Before the war, I had been living in London with my mother. I was 15, nearly 16, in my fifth year at Eton I believe, and I had made many friends, I was happy. My father had died in the Great War but left my mother a great fortune to live off. His parents had been steel merchants in the US at the end of the 19th century and had sold their company for a considerable amount of money to a railroad builder on the west coast of Nevada, as far as I recall. Anyway. My mother was a wonderful woman, clever and fun. She loved nice things and would always treat me extremely well, but I will have you know she could be very sensible and savvy with her investments as well, and eventually doubled my father's fortune in the years after his death. She was also extremely magnanimous and often contributed to the poor and gave generous amounts of money to charities. Anyway, I digress. I had established myself at Eaton and, as I said, made many friends. I liked to think I was quite popular with students and teachers alike, and I also studied hard. I had a keen interest in mathematics and the sciences, and as a result wanted to eventually become a physicist, something I never quite achieved, unfortunately.

My mother had always loved the sea, and my father would take her twice a year to Weymouth on the Dorset Coast, where they would stay in a bed and breakfast very close to the local beach and enjoy a week's holiday together. Now that my father had passed away, she longed for the beach and the holidays she used to have with Papa. So, during one summer break from school, I reluctantly offered to accompany her to her favourite spot, so she would not have to go alone. Now you must understand that I had made plans to stay at my friend Monty's Berkshire estate. I was going for several weeks, so I changed my plans and ended up venturing to the south coast with my ever so jubilant mother. And I'll be honest. To begin with, I was not a happy chap, the thought of missing out on all the fun and larks I would have with my chums. But after seeing my mother this cock-a-hoop about me agreeing to join her I had to concede it was worth the sacrifice. I hadn't seen her this happy for many years."

Bryson pauses for a quiet moment of reflection, remembering his mother's beaming smile when he had broken the news to her.

"Our chauffer drove us from our flat in Kensington through London and out into the lush English countryside. I remember my annoyance at missing out on spending the summer with my friends dissipating, as both my mother and I chatted and laughed with each other, occasionally looking out the window to see the small, picturesque towns we would pass through, our driver occasionally announcing the names of these wonderful places. I believe he had taken it upon himself to become our own personal tour guide for the day.

Bryson then stops his story to adjust his voice, attempting an amusing imitation, "Winchester Ma'am, Dorchester Ma'am, lavily little taan's if I do say so miself", he then says in his best south London accent. Nancy laughs, and then Bryson, pleased with himself at the comedic addition to his story. He gathers himself by clearing his throat and continues.

"We drove for hours, passing field after field. Just as I was going to suggest to my mother we stop for the evening at a quaint little B&B we had not long passed by, I opened my window and finally, the sea! I could smell it before I could see it. It was invigorating; just to know we were close filled us both with such excitement.

We pulled in at the Crown Hotel around 5.30ish in the evening. It was situated just on the edge of town. Mother always said how clean it was and how good the breakfast was, so she refused to stay at any of the grander hotels in town. "This is perfectly sufficient," she would say, "what more could we need?", and she was right, as usual. After unpacking, we had decided to take a walk on the beach before supper, so we took the pathway from the hotel, a mere 200 metres, give or take, if my memory serves me right, but it was a long time ago, Nancy, you must remember." Bryson stops again, his eyes squinting in concentration as he searches for the memories. Nancy is still sitting on the stool, entranced by the story being told to her.

"My mother and I walked along the beach, taking in the fresh sea air, beguiling in the dusky evening, and admiring the red, orange, and lilac sun setting over the horizon, myself strolling along the beach taking in the ambience of this serene and halcyon place, my playful mother, as if regressed to her childhood, paddling in the shallow water, occasionally jumping over waves she feared would splash on to her dress. It was peace on a primarily capricious Earth. We walked past a row of bathing machines with families, hurriedly queuing and changing in an attempt to return to their accommodation in town or home before the traffic. As I walked on a bit further past the bathers, Mother just ahead collecting shells, I spotted someone amongst the marram grass on top of a small dune. There, soaking in the remaining light of the day, sat a boy, mesmeric and exquisite. He was the most beauteous thing I had ever seen. Easel and canvas placed precariously in front of him, brush in his right hand and pallet in the left, his eyes looking out upon the apparent horizon, concentration, then a change of focus to his canvas, then back again to analyse his next stroke. Nancy, I had to stop. My heart was quite literally paralysed for a second. I felt it stop. It was like nothing I had ever experienced." Bryson smiles. He looks at the painting and squeezes Nancy's hand, then lifts his right hand to his chest, feeling the vehemence return.

"My mother, ever the art enthusiast, had already made her way across the beach and up the dune to investigate what this enchanting young man was painting, embarrassing as you can imagine, Nancy. I waited on the beach a while, watching them chat occasionally and attempting to pensively look out to sea. I looked over quickly to see them pointing at something. I also saw he must have said something humorous, because my mother laughed hysterically at one point. Poor woman, for all her great attributes, she had a terribly awful laugh, almost seagull-like, 'a repetitive squawk' I remember someone had playfully described it as. Anyway, I am attempting to mind my own business and wait quietly on the beach when I hear my mother shouting to me to join them. I glance over again and spot her sitting next to her new acquaintance with a glass of red wine. Oh, I could have died, Nancy, but what could I do? I meandered up the dune quite ungracefully to my mother and her new artist friend.

On arrival, I was greeted with a small hock full of red wine and my mother already filling her second glass. I shyly introduced myself and obviously apologised for my mother to the man who had quite visibly enchanted her and had quite unintentionally enchanted me. He told me his name was Elijah, and that my mother and I were now the proud owners of a freshly painted seascape, and that she was one of the most charming women he had ever met, which I had to agree with despite her laugh.

Oh, but the painting, Nancy. It was like nothing I'd ever seen before. I had initially thought the purchase of the painting by my mother was a charitable gesture, but you could see that his eye for colour and depth was incomparable. My mother and I looked at each other, knowing we had found something and someone very special. We sat and drank with this young man for several hours, and I was captivated by him. Elijah was 19 years old at the time we met him. He was originally from Brighton, the product of an English father and Dutch mother who had fallen in love during the war. His mother was of Jewish heritage and had been saved by Elijah's father. Elijah had recently returned to England after travelling around Europe and North Africa. His experiences were otherworldly. He told stories with such exuberance and life, he told us of places and people we had never dreamt to go or meet, my mother and I could not move, engrossed, and allured by every tale he told. We sat listening and talking with Elijah for hours. It was the most wonderful evening I'd ever had, but of course, eventually, the wine ran dry and my mother hit her proverbial wall and fell asleep on the beach. I of course decided it was time to escort her home, but before I could say anything about leaving, Elijah continued to talk, he was so relaxed and funny but had an intensity about him. It was exciting and inspiring, but most of all it induced something inside me. I couldn't leave yet. Elijah told me he had seen me walking down the beach before I spotted him. He said that he had seen me look over to him and he had seen me stop. I was frozen, Nancy, but my body was awash with rapture.

Elijah then moved off his stool, where he had been sitting all evening, legs crossed, occasionally imbibing wine directly from the bottle after topping up our glasses. He moved slowly, never taking his eyes from mine, and eventually sat on the soft, cold sand beside me. We stayed there for a while before he gently brought his hand up from off the ground, stroking my neck, his fingers undoing the top buttons of my shirt… then…. A kiss, soft and sweet, I didn't know… it was… it was..." Bryson stops and takes a breath.

"Are you ok, my love? You don't have to continue, obviously we don't want you getting upset, do we?" Nancy says, concerned with the manner in which Bryson had stopped his story.

"No! I must continue!" Bryson replies. There is a sharpness and determination to his voice. "Sorry Nancy, I mean, I want to continue. I need to. This story is for both of us. Please just continue to hold my hand, and I'll be fine." He smiles at her, but Nancy is still concerned. She squeezes his hand once again.

"Continue, Bryson, but please stop if it becomes too much," she responds. Bryson looks up at the painting and then closes his eyes. He sees Elijah's hair sweeping in the breeze. He remembers his ocean smell and his salty lips, his soft sun-kissed skin, and the tiny sunspots scattered on his face.

"Elijah asked if he could meet me again the following day and I, of course, agreed, then escorted my extremely tired and drunk mother back to our hotel a bit further down the beach." Bryson stops and chuckles to himself. "I remember my mother. On the way back, I mean, she kept saying how lovely Elijah was and what a wonderful evening she'd had. I, of course, had to agree with her.

The following morning, my mother and I had breakfast together and then a stroll into town so she could browse the shops and then have an early lunch. By the afternoon, Mother was tired, so I told her I would meet Elijah and collect our painting, to which she agreed. My mother had generously offered six pounds for the picture, which, I can tell you, was a huge amount of money in those days, Nancy. Elijah had refused to accept, but Mother had insisted, she was like that... Anyway, I went back to the place we had met the night before, and there again was Elijah. My tummy fluttered as I drew closer. I could see he was adding the finishing touches to my mother's painting; it was worth every penny my mother paid. I had visited many galleries with my mother in London, and I just knew this painting was special. Elijah again had his supply of wine and had brought cigarettes for us, so obviously, we drank the afternoon away.

I felt so comfortable with him, I felt more myself than I had ever been in my life. Even after our kiss the previous evening, we were both at ease with each other. Occasionally, when the beach was less busy, he would stroke the palm and back of my hand with his fingers. It was exciting and dangerous. This sort of thing was very taboo then, as you can imagine. I realised that the sun was setting, and Mother would be wondering where I had been all afternoon, so I told Elijah I had to go. He begged me to stay, but I had Mother to think about. As I was about to leave, I had an idea. I realised my room's balcony was extremely accessible via a fire escape near the hotel kitchen and that perhaps Elijah could meet me there later that evening, so I asked him, but I said he could only come as long as he brought some more wine for us." Bryson pauses and a little smile appears in the corner of his mouth.

Nancy can barely contain herself. "So what did he say?"

Bryson turns to her, a look of slight disbelief in his eye. "My dear, he told me that he could think of no place in the world he'd rather be than in that room with me." He turns back to the painting and continues.

"I had dinner with Mother, who had slept off her hangover. I seem to remember the old bat was a bottle and a half of Beaujolais down before dessert that evening," Bryson says comically, and both Nancy and Bryson laugh. "I returned to my room once I knew Mother was asleep, then lay on my bed until I heard a knock at the window. I had been attempting to read my book, but in reality, I was just wondering what was to come that evening, as you can imagine Nancy. I looked up at the window to see this angel, the light of the moon dancing off his beautiful locks. I had to take a second to behold this beautiful creature I saw before me. He had, as promised, brought two bottles of wine. We only managed to drink one, though. The wait was too much for both of us. Elijah guided me over to the bed, laid me down, and changed my life forever. It was without fail the most magical night of my life.

We saw each other every night after that, and sometimes we would steal a few hours in the day for walks, or I would sit with Elijah while he painted, exchanging playful glances. Oh, how we laughed! He was incredibly funny, Nancy. His wit was so sharp and worldly. My mother actually invited him for dinner one evening. I remember it was with some friends of hers who were holidaying there as well, and myself, of course. One of the guests was a rather charming but pompous man named Alistair Monroe–Stephens. He had said after seeing some of Elijah's paintings, "Well, you're more beautiful than I and more talented, but at least I'm wealthier," to which Elijah responded, "Well sir, how is it you know this? I may be the full package, faultless perhaps." His naughty smile confirmed his joke. Everyone thought he was a hoot, so cultured and clever for a boy of his age. He offered to paint Mr and Mrs Monroe–Stephens for free. I remember he had said what a handsome couple they were. They were extremely flattered, as you can imagine, Nancy. He was such a success at dinner, they paid him rather well for the painting if my memory serves me right.

When the last day of my holiday came around, we arranged to meet on the beach that night. We drank, we made love, and we held each other for what felt like an eternity. He told me that he loved me. I remember him telling me we would never be closer to the end than we were at this moment, and if he were to die tomorrow, he would be happy just knowing that I knew how much I meant to him. He then gave me a painting to remember us by, the painting you see before you." Bryson stops. He begins to cry, a soft choking but uncontrollable sob. Others from around the room look over to see what is happening, but eventually go back to their activities.

Nancy squeezes Bryson's hand. "So, you and Elijah are the boys in the painting? He did that for you?" she feels herself start to give in to her emotions but holds back only for the sake of the man sitting next to her. "You're the boy on the left, aren't you? You're watching Elijah."

Bryson, now managing to compose himself slightly, looks at the painting again. "No, my dear, that is Elijah. He is the one watching me. This painting is an everlasting symbol of his love for me. I am the boy throwing the stone, and he is the one longing for me. This is how he saw me."

Nancy looks at the painting once again, and she sees Elijah, his blonde hair and sun-kissed skin, just as he'd been described. She sees the look in his eyes, the adoration for the younger version of Bryson, the absolute devotion and reverence that only comes from love.

"Bryson, what happened after?" Nancy asks fervently.

Bryson now begins to speak more matter-of-factly, a mist of anger about his voice. "We wrote to each other every week without fail. We said how we would travel together and how he would come and see me and my mother in London. Then, around six months after returning home, I stopped receiving his letters. I was worried and confided in my mother, who by this time was aware of my situation with Elijah. Liberal as she was, it was a worry for her. It didn't help that she was at this point heavily intoxicated most of the time with her new husband Roger. I begged her to let me return, but all she would say was that love comes along more than once, and the time I had spent with Elijah was special, but I had to move on with my life. But I knew something was adrift, and my determination finally got the better of her, so one weekend we took the car back to Weymouth.

On arrival, I ran to the spot where I had first seen Elijah painting our picture, then to every other spot on the beach where I had met him or seen him painting, but no Elijah. I returned to the hotel, where Mother was waiting with her friend, the owner, Christine. She was comforting my mother. They told me Elijah had gotten drunk one night and drowned in the ocean a few miles up the beach. They had found his body the next morning. I of course instantly knew this was a lie and angrily stormed away. I just knew that was something he wouldn't let happen to himself. Later that day I spoke to one of the maids who had befriended Elijah and me on my visit. She all but confirmed he had been beaten and dumped by some of the local boys after they had found out about his sexuality, but obviously, there was no proof." Bryson sits quietly. He stares at the wall beneath the picture, reflecting on the events in his life.

Nancy looks at him intently. "I'm so sorry, I'm so sorry you had to go through that. You were so young, just a boy really," she says, striving to find some comforting words.

Bryson, now stern and matter of fact, continues. "Two months later, I was raped and beaten by my stepfather. My mother found out soon afterwards and subsequently killed herself, but not before dousing him in brandy and setting him alight in our living room. The house burnt to ashes, both of them inside. She felt guilty for bringing him into our life. I never blamed her. She was, like Elijah, one of the great loves of my life, and she loved me for who I was and who I am. See, Nancy. This is for you. If you can take anything from this story, I want it to be that finding true love is the most paramount thing in life. It's not something a lot of people find, my dear. I guarantee this. I tell you this because we have an understanding. This thing we call love is a gift, and I will never lose this gift. I will never misplace or replace it, because it is a part of me. It is the greatest part of me. I want you to remember that loss is a part of life, and we must all try at least to find the strength to continue the best we can, because no one survives this life without some semblance of loss."

Nancy looks at Bryson, her eyes narrow. Pensively, she absorbs these words. Bryson retreats, and his tone changes. He has suddenly transformed into another person. "Oh Nancy, I am an old fuddy-duddy. I've been sitting here talking away about myself, my sad old stories. I just want some of these poor souls to get out and on with their lives, not stuck in this place, you know? What's the point of a hospital if the people in it don't heal? I haven't even asked how you are. I have it on good authority that you're taking your beautiful family to the beach this weekend. That sounds glorious. Where will you go, my dear?

Chapter 14 – The Lost Boy

13.3 March 1977

As the music played, Nancy stared at the rooves of the neat Victorian terraced houses across the road, lost in her reverie, oblivious to the lives and events that surround her and passed her by. She had not heard anything as beautiful for many years, maybe not ever. The bench on which she sat was damp, but she had sat down regardless, the moisture that had set into the wood seeping through her sky-blue jeans. There was no breeze, but the air was crisp on Nancy's face. She was daydreaming about nothing, entranced by the heavenly notes that she could hear faintly dancing into her mind.

She looked at the man on the opposite side of the road and saw the source of the music. His long grey beard was almost touching the strings of the violin, his eyes closed tightly, his bow delicately stroking each string, the rich and fluid music gently travelled across the narrow road to the pavement, then the bench where Nancy had somehow found herself. Her weary eyes looked at the dark clouds clearing overhead, her mind lost in the music, one hand on her daughter growing inside her, whom she couldn't wait to meet.

A few moments of tranquillity, the music and the peace, and nothing more.

Then it happened, a paralysing strike of worry overcame Nancy. A Ford Cortina had sped by, splashing up water over her shins, Pink Floyd's 'Wish you were here' blared from the car speakers. Nancy's eyes blurred as her mind resumed normality; something wasn't right. Nancy looked at the empty spaces on each side of the bench, at the shopping centre down the main street to her right, then at the crossroads on her left. Where was Henry? Where was her son? Where had she last seen him?

She stood up with urgency, racking her brain, retracing her movements from the previous hour, memories of where she had been flooding back to her like waves, one, then another, then another. She remembered she had been to the supermarket for dinner, then to the pharmacy for some medication for Jonathan, then to the shopping centre.

She walked, uncomfortably but quickly and anxiously, towards the shopping centre, holding her stomach to protect the one child that was still with her, asking passers-by if they had seen Henry, describing him frantically, but to no avail.

She ran past the rows of shops lining the road either side of her, moving around the ornamental plants down the middle of the concourse, still asking passers-by if they had seen a little boy. A middle-aged woman with a teenage boy had overheard the commotion and approached Nancy. She said she had seen a young boy alone in 'Pete's Pets', the old pet shop on the edge of the shopping centre. Nancy remembered going in as a girl and how badly it smelt.

As she entered 'Pete's Pets', she saw an old man sitting reading the paper. She recognised him from her childhood, with his wispy moustache and long receding hair. Although older, he was the same as Nancy remembered. He didn't even look up to see Nancy franticly walk in. "Sir, I mean Mr Collins, have you seen my son? He's nine years old with dark brown hair. Someone said they may have seen him here." Nancy's head darted around the room in search of her son.

Pete looked up at Nancy, then turned his head to the door, recalling the customers he had seen earlier in the day, mild concern in his eyes. "There was a family in earlier looking at the parrot, love, but I don't think I've seen a boy here." He stopped and thought again. "No... I really don't think so, but feel free to look around, though. I'll keep an eye out for him from the window. He may be wandering about the shopping centre outside. Don't panic though, there's always police and security about, so he'll get found, lass."

Although she thought the man was initially going to be hard to deal with, she was comforted by his growing concern.

"Thank you very much. I'll take a look if that's ok, just to be sure he's not hiding somewhere. He does like to hide sometimes," Nancy replied, already turning to look around the shop, bending to check under shelves and round corners.

"No problem. I'm sure he'll turn up. As I said, there's lots of people around. Someone will take care of him while…"

Nancy heard the words fade as she briskly walked to the back of the shop past the strongly smelling foods for various animals, gerbils and mice scurrying around their cages, scared at every slight noise they heard and new face they saw. She noticed the parrot he had mentioned moments before, large and old-looking, a solemn king amongst its tiny subjects shuffling around in cages on either side of his large courtly cage.

"Shit, he's not here," Nancy remarked to herself, still checking under shelves.

"Shit he's not here… quark, quark," repeated the parrot.

She stopped briefly and looked at the parrot again. Slightly shocked, she walked away, still looking along aisles and in hiding places fit for little boys, past the rabbits and guinea pigs, until she was almost out of the store.

"In my dream, I killed her dead… quark."

Nancy stopped and looked back at the parrot that was now looking directly at her, its head tilting momentarily to one side a few times and then to the other, repeating the process. Nancy's eyes narrowed then widened as she looked in wonder. She attempted to speak but ended up mumbling.

"My name's Henry, what's yours? Quark," the bird said out of nowhere.

"What?" Nancy coughed. She looked at the man behind the counter, who was still looking out the window to see if Henry might pass. "Did you hear that? Did you hear what your parrot just said?" she barked, flustered, and confused.

"Hear what? He's always talking rubbish, that bird," he answered, turning to look at Nancy. "Your boy's not here, love. You'd be better out there in the lobby. That's where he'll more than likely be."

"But your bird said… it said." Nancy paused and realised the man wouldn't necessarily be interested in anything she said. "I have to go, thank you for your help."

Nancy had now become increasingly flustered; her optimism that Henry might be safe was rapidly waning.

Now out of ideas, Nancy left the mall, intending to see if Henry had been taken to the police station close to where she had been sitting on the bench previously, her mind was clouded, switching from despair to hope intermittently.

As she walked towards the station, she heard something.

"Mummy! Mummy! I'm here, I'm over here!" a voice yelled in her direction.

"Henry! Henry!" Nancy screamed before seeing him. There, sitting on the bench she had been on only 15 minutes before, was her son. He was holding a violin and a bow, attempting to play a song. Next to him was the old musician that had enchanted her. They were talking calmly, like old friends. Henry was smiling at him as the violin man talked calmly to him.

"Thank you so much for looking after my son," Nancy said with the last of her breath. "I was… I was so very worried."

"Ay, t'was no problem, my dear. We had a lovely chat, didn't we Henry?"

Henry smiled at the man but did not look at his mother. He continued to play the violin, his face in a trance of concentration.

Nancy began to cry with relief. "I was so worried about him; I don't know what happened," she sobbed to the old man.

"I saw him wandering o yonder, up the street, outside the shopping centre so just wanted to be sure he was ok. I used to have a daughter, but she died long ago, t'was way back when I lived in Ireland."

Nancy wondered at the relevance of what the man had just said to her but decided not to delve any further.

"Oh ok, I am sorry to hear that, and I do really appreciate what you did here today. God knows what would have happened, so I'm truly grateful to you. Can I give you anything? Some money? Food, perhaps?"

The old man sat quietly on the bench for a moment, looking at her intently, then stood up. He stood beside Nancy, his head arched in her direction, he stared directly at her, his eyes narrowing and widening. Nancy began to feel uncomfortable as she realised his unusual behaviour. This man then, without notice, turned to her, grabbing her hand in the process. It was not vicious, but Nancy does not see it coming and thus did not have time to pull away.

Then the old man spoke quietly but earnestly to Nancy, "God is not here today, Nancy, you must see that when you decide to step into your future the enemy will always be there… He will hound you and he will assail you, reminding you of your past… If you resist the Devil, HE. SHALL. FLEE!"

Nancy finally pulled her hand away and took a step back from the old man. She began to shake; a state of shock overcame her.

"Wha… I'm not sure I understand what you mean, sir, I think maybe you should go…" But before Nancy could finish her reply, face scrunched and puzzled, the old man had walked away down the path, taking a right and disappearing down the alley behind the old bookstore, all within seconds, without even a glance back, leaving Nancy, Henry, and his violin on the bench where she had blissfully sat not so long ago.

14 Chapter 15 – Fears and Demons

14.1 February 1979

Nancy looks intently at her husband as he climbs into bed next to her. "Today was a strange day, my darling. I attended the funeral of one of my patients, a sad situation. This woman, she was a patient of mine, but she was also my friend, one of those people that shouldn't have been there. The ones I've told you about before."

Jonathan, attempting to be as empathetic as ever, leans in close to his wife. "I'm sorry to hear that love, are you ok? Death is a strange thing as you know darling, it affects us all differently," he says, not quite knowing the right words.

Nancy continues to talk, her contemplative state semi-ignoring her unhelpful husband. "Her sister was the only family member to attend, in the whole world, no one else, aside from me and the girls, she was the only person to turn up." Nancy can feel herself getting upset, but she manages to conceal it. "I don't really understand, if her sister loved her that much, then why didn't she do someth…?" Nancy stops herself again, feeling the indignation within her swell. Jonathan watches his wife; his curiosity increases as her mood changes, and she falls deeper into thought. "She… the sister I mean, she, she had a book, it was called The Little White Horse… I think perhaps Margaret and her sister would read it together as children, maybe. That's nice I suppose. She dropped it on the coffin during the funeral and then left the hospital. It's sad, but at least she turned up, I suppose. I have to give her that."

The couple sits for a moment in silence. Jonathan looks at his wife, visibly sad and exhausted. She inevitably starts to weep, and he gently moves in towards her until he is comforting her in his arms. She calms herself, and they sit together for a while, quietly.

Jonathan thinks about his wife and his children, he thinks about his son, and he thinks of the pain he has caused them. Finally, he finds the words for his grieving wife. "Sometimes we bury our fears and the demons that haunt us. Sometimes we choose to remain ignorant of the world. It's a coping mechanism so that we don't feel the pain of losing the ones we love."

She smiles wryly. "Sometimes you're too clever, my darling." She kisses him and returns to her position in his arms. "Thank you for listening," Nancy coos.

Jonathan's eyes close. He rests back on the mounded pillows behind him. His mind drifts away, and in a trance, the last words he can muster are, "Anytime, Nancy, I hope you know how much I love you darling".

Nancy tries to relax and forget about the day's events by unwinding into sleep. Suddenly, she remembers something. "While at the funeral today, I saw a woman in the top window watching the funeral. Her face was familiar, but it wasn't clear enough for me to see. I rubbed the tears from my eyes to try to clear my vision, but she had already gone. It's a face I can't shake from my mind." But Jonathan is already asleep and doesn't hear. Nancy turns out the lamp and she, in turn, drifts into a slumber of her own, forgetting about the woman in the window and the pain of the day.

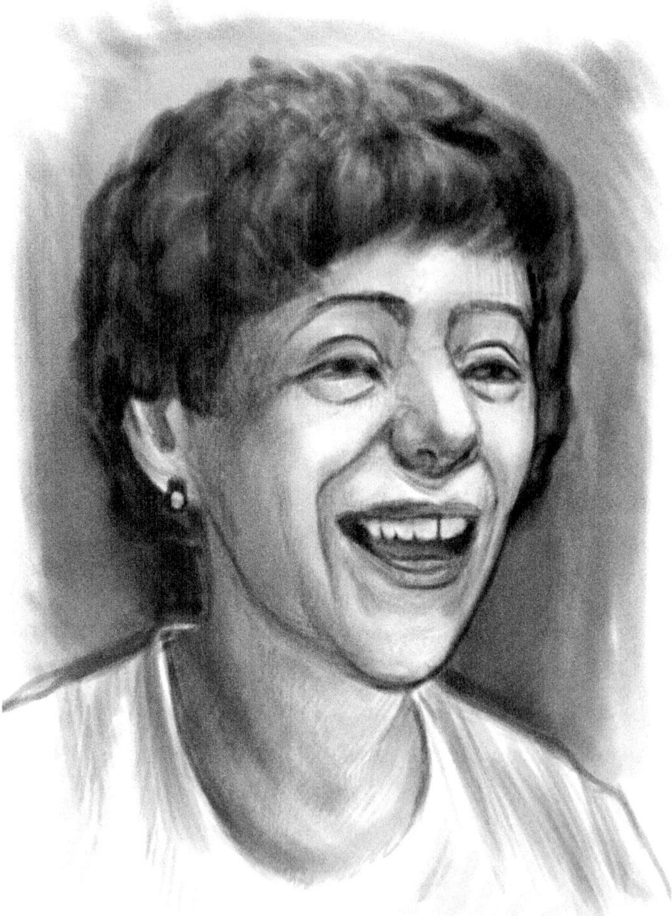

15 Chapter 16 – The Group Session

15.1 March 1984 – Present day

As the day ends, Nancy is working hard in the laundry. Only an hour now until she can leave. Val has snuck off early to do some shopping for her daughter's birthday, and Nancy is happy to cover for her friend. She finds it relaxing to wind down her shift folding towels and sheets. Her mind races with thoughts of her children and husband; sometimes she sings and sometimes she hums to songs she makes up on the spot. She smells the fresh sheets in her hands and thinks about her day, chatting with Val and joking with the patients.

After a while, Val and Andrea begin to chat with each other about different goings-on in the hospital. They like to chat with each other, and Nancy enjoys listening to their conversations. She likes to see them happy and jovial; she can observe them both, knowing that they are still safe and close to her. "I thought you had gone home, Val, and I thought you were not feeling well today, Andrea love, you called in earlier?" Nancy realises that she was completely unaware that both Val and Andrea were in the room with her until that point.

Andrea stops talking and immediately looks at Nancy, face scrunched up, like a parent preparing to scold a child, eyes narrowed, and head tipped to one side. "Well, Nancy, my dear, we're here to see you of course and give you a hand finishing these sheets and clothes you have to finish today. We've been watching you, and it's clear you've been struggling lately. We want to help you in any way we can."

Nancy smiles at her two friends. "Yes, I have a bit. I'm not entirely sure why though," she replies as she looks down and continues folding the pillowcase she is holding.

"We've chatted so much today, Nancy, but I didn't think to ask how you are. How are you, love? How are things? Do you ever still think about your dad?" Val asks, now standing with a comforting hand on her friend's back.

Nancy thinks this is an odd question and is a little bit shocked, but this was a question that she had wanted someone to ask her for a long time. "I still think about him sometimes, I suppose. Quite a lot. To be honest, I see him in my dreams more than anything else. Many dreams, but the most common dream I have, about him I mean, is very strange. He is cuddling me in our kitchen, in our old house I mean. He is holding me very tight so that I can't release myself from his grip, I try to but he's too strong, so I stay holding him in turn because I feel his pain. He is whispering to me that he's sorry, and 'everything will be ok in the end'. He says he will see me again in the end and 'the crying hour is nearly over'. He repeats this… over and over and over until I finally wake up. It's so real I can almost feel his breath on my cheek."

Nancy stops folding a blue-striped shirt and touches the side of her face with the tips of her fingers. The shirt unfolds and falls to her side, hanging like a child from her hand.

Andrea and Val look at each other with puzzled expressions, then back at Nancy, their heads moving in perfect tandem, left then right then upright. "What do you think this means, Nancy?" says Andrea.

Nancy perches herself on the stool where the seamstress normally sits but has since finished for the day. She mulls over this question for a short while. "I'm not sure. I suppose he is watching over me in a way, I would guess, I can't really work it out," Nancy muses to herself.

"Maybe he's preparing you for something? Maybe this is what he's trying to tell you," Val says pensively before they hear footsteps in the corridor outside.

Nancy hears the laundry door slowly open behind her. She turns her head slightly to see a nurse entering the room and closing the door gently behind her.

Nancy continues to fold the remaining laundry methodically, unaffected by her visitor. "Hello, Nancy, how're you getting on? I can see you're nearly finished. Remember that it's group therapy this evening, so I'll see you in the little living room in ten, ok? Try not to be late."

Nancy, without turning, responds agreeably, "Yes, of course, I completely forgot, see you in ten." She hears the door close, and the nurse walks slowly down the long corridor connecting the east side to the west side of the building, her echoing steps gradually becoming more and more distant until finally, there's silence again. Nancy puts down the top sheet she is folding and takes a breath. A twitch of doubt runs through her body. She is at once quite confused. She did not recognise the nurse. How very odd, she thought. Nancy knew all the staff here at the hospital; she made it her duty to befriend any newcomer and always tried to help them settle in. She knew how daunting it could be. Maybe this girl was new? She thought, "It must be one of the 'Subbies', brought in when they were understaffed! Yes! That's it, how silly." Nancy mumbles to herself as she folds the last remaining sheet and heads out the door. Down the long corridor, her slippers are muffled on the concrete floor as she heads to the living room.

Nancy enters the little living room, where four patients and the nurse who had previously reminded her of the session all sit, waiting patiently for Nancy before they can begin. An empty seat is waiting for her next to the nurse from the laundry, whom Nancy now recognised but could not for the life of her put a name to. Nancy sits finally and continues to rack her brain, Nurse... Nurse Something. What is it? Maybe Johnson or Jansen, she ponders for a while, but in vain. She comforts herself with the fact that introductions will be done soon and then she will know whom she is working with. Nancy takes the empty seat next to her colleague and adjusts her body so as to be as comfortable as possible.

"Ok, shall we begin? My name is Nurse Burton..."

"And I'm Nurse Blake," Nancy quickly interrupts.

"Thank you, Nancy," says Nurse Burton with a slightly aggrieved-to-be-interrupted tone, but also a strangely sympathetic smile that she directs to Nancy immediately after.

The group consists of Debbie Flint, Jayne Cobb, Bryson Collins, and Richard Moore. Richard was an American who had only arrived at the hospital a few months earlier. Although he obviously had issues and an acute nervous disposition, he seemed very slightly more normal than the other patients. Nancy had been told he had attended four years of medical school in the US before dropping out and moving to the UK. Nancy didn't know what to think of the young man sitting opposite her. She had thought they had initially got on well, but one spring afternoon while walking in the gardens, she had heard him speaking to one of the junior nurses about her. She had heard Richard quietly say that he wasn't sure she should still be a nurse, and that the techniques used by Nancy didn't help the other patients or herself. Nancy was horrified that a patient had criticised how she did her job to other people, a job she had done for 15 years. She had told Val, who agreed it was out of order, but warned her not to upset the apple cart and not to get angry. She was the nurse, and he was the patient, and that was all that mattered.

"As you're all aware, we hold these group sessions each day at five pm. It is an opportunity for you all to talk about anything and everything, to vent any frustrations and receive feedback from the nurses and your peers. Ok Richard, would you like to start? You were very quiet yesterday, I remember," Nurse Burton continues to Richard with a rather fake sincerity to her voice. Everyone is quiet for a second.

Debbie, ever the comedienne of the group, mutters so everyone can hear, "What's the point, crazy people talk, and no one listens."

Richard is very skinny, nervous, mid-to-late-twenties, Nancy guesses, from his wiser demeanour. His eyes dart around the room like a nervous animal looking for an escape. Eye contact was not something he seemed capable of at any time, let alone this moment. He would transition from a disturbing smile to a petrified state of nervousness, his smile changing to absolute fear and back again.

"Are you going to talk to us today, Richard? This is a safe place, as you know. If you have something to say you can, if not we can try again tomorrow, but you know how much better you feel when you open up, don't you?" Another dose of encouragement from Nurse Burton seems to do the trick, and she looks at him directly, trying to meet his eyes with hers. She is much more attentive now, her demeanour almost begging for a response.

"Yes, Nurse Burton," Richard replies softly while looking everywhere and at everyone else in the room except her. "Ok... Well... Ummm... I... Ummm... as I have said before... I think... Maybe... I think just, well maybe I didn't, I don't know, I can't remember now, but... Maybe I did, so I grew up in a foster home, you know? In care... Do you know what I mean? ... Yes, of course, you do... I am being silly, I am sorry. Well. While I was there... some people... I mean the people who cared for me and the others, well they were supposed to care for me and them, the others I mean, well, they would sort of.... Well, they sort of... Ummm." Richard stops. He takes a moment and manages to settle himself slightly. His nervous disposition changes, and he becomes slightly calmer and more focused. "Umm, well, what I am trying to say is that, well, these people did terrible things to me and, well, the other people they were supposed to care for. They took advantage of children at their most vulnerable, boys and girls, scared and wondering what they might have done to deserve such torment." Richard stops and looks at the ceiling in order to finish his monologue. "I am continuously haunted by it and haunted by my friends who never made it out that place alive, and although these people are gone, either locked away or now in the darkest depths of the most disgusting parts of hell... well..." Richard then tilts his head forward, eyes wide, staring directly at Nancy. "I fear this blackness that follows me, from room to room, and from minute to minute, from second to second, will never, ever, leave me alone".

The room is silent for a while aside from the scratching of Nurse Burton's pen against the paper clipped on her cork clipboard. Nancy is sitting quietly. She feels a change in the room. She is calm despite Richard's strange behaviour. She assesses the patients around her, taking in their faces, some sad, some emotionless and some perfectly happy to be there.

Nancy gauges the room and decides to get the group talking again. "Jayne, would you like to go next? I believe it's been a while since you've contributed to a group session." She smiles at Jayne, the same smile that Nurse Burton had given Richard moments before, fake sincerity oozing from every word. Jayne looks up and glances at Nancy, her eyes narrow with a degree of dislike, worse, contempt—a look almost of lingering disgust that everyone can see. Nancy cannot understand why.

Jayne shakes her head side to side very slowly, and then she looks over at Nurse Burton with a very evident disapproving smirk. "Nurse Burton, I don't believe these sessions are going to be very effective if Nancy is nominating us all to speak again. I find it hugely stressful, and as you know, stress is the last thing I need right now. What with everything going on in my head, you know I have issues with her talking to me like I'm fucking mentally retarded. Why doesn't Nancy speak for once? You all walk on eggshells around her and I'm tired of it. We've all had ghastly and awful things happen in our lives. That's why most of us are here. We've just heard as much from poor Richard, so what..."

Before Jayne could say another word Nurse Burton interrupts, "Umm, I think that's enough, Jayne. Nancy will speak when she is good and ready, and I have told you that you can't just..."

Jayne, not one to be interrupted, then loudly starts to speak over Nurse Burton, "I concur, Nancy's situation is terrible, I really do sympathise, we all do, I'm sure, and I honestly can't imagine what it's like to have gone through the trauma she's been through, I mean to have that happen to your family, I couldn't live with myself…"

Nurse Burton, now with rising anger, interrupts again. "Jayne! Stop! That is quite enough."

Nancy sits silently. The room is quiet again. She sees faces looking at her and uniforms she doesn't recognise. Confusion sets in. Are these her memories? Are they real? What is this place? The faces begin to blur, the people around her look fuzzy, as though she is seeing them through teary eyes. She sees the world, but it's not her world. She looks at the clock, a clock she has never seen before. "Is that clock new? I can't think if I've seen it before," Nancy says under her breath, eyes fixed on nothing but the clock. She notices the second-hand ticks but never moves, it ticks and ticks, but remains on the 10th second continuously, just a slight shudder of the hand as each second passes, but never moving, stuck in that moment eternally. Nancy notices a shadow move over her; it is Nurse Burton.

"Are you ok, Nancy? Would you like to go back to your room? Please take no notice of Jayne. Maybe we can get your photo albums out again later. We love looking at pictures of your girls, don't we?" Then, like a lightbulb in an old factory, disused and abandoned for years, finally something clicks, she is back, she remembers everything.

She remembers waking up strapped to her bed, unable to move her body, in a room full of screaming patients. She remembers turning her head so she can see the sunshine stream in and seeing her family in every beam that warmed her face.

She remembers being led by two nurses to the breakfast room, and how they were chatting with each other about their lives outside the hospital. She remembers how much she wanted to join their conversation and tell them about her family and how she would see them that night, but never got the opportunity.

She remembers eating breakfast alone and talking to the ghosts that surrounded her, her friends she had lost, Val and Andrea, both now long dead.

She remembers mornings of medication and taking part in the music and art sessions with her fellow patients, helping them with each paintbrush stroke and seeing their beautiful paintings.

She remembers helping Nurse Burton change the rooms and do the laundry, and how when she saw the empty graveyard opposite the hospital she was taken back to memories of Margaret, her friend and patient, and her solemn funeral.

She remembers watching a new episode of her husband's television show—a show he was no part of anymore.

She remembers her patients, no... she remembers these people who surround her, she remembers these are not her patients, they are the same as her, dressed in gowns and slippers, she is the patient, and they are her co-patients.

She remembers everything.

As these horrors unravel before her, Nancy falls sidewards from her chair, and she hits the floor paralysed. The ceiling becomes black and turns to dust, she is drowning in her own ashes, and she is drowning in the ashes of her family. The nurses attending, Nurse Burton and Nurse Appleby, hold Nancy down as she begins to have a fit. Her body twitches every few seconds with such force, Nurse Burton is thrown onto her side, and she hits her right eye on the cold laminate flooring.

"This is the worse one she's had so far, Sarah, just keep hold of her so she doesn't hurt herself." Sarah Appleby had been working at Peacock Street for only a few months and was clearly panicking. Three other nurses run in as Nurse Burton manages to administer a sedative just as Nancy begins to convulse.

Nancy stops moving, but her wailing continues, harrowingly echoing around the room as she is lifted into a wheelchair, then carted down the long corridor connecting the living quarters to the dining room and TV room, locked bedrooms on either side, small windows with eyes peering into a world beyond their bedrooms, confused at what's happening, disturbed by the commotion. Nancy has an awakening, the screams of the patients around her echo the screams of her family.

The crying hour has begun, and the world around Nancy becomes very suddenly dark as she remembers more of what had been…

She remembers those moments of her life she had tried to forget, the memories she had locked away, locked away in the furthest ether of her mind, the key now turned, the fiery gate open.

16 Chapter 17 – The Revelation

16.1 July 1982

"Mum, Mum! Listen to me, you really must be quiet now," Henry calmly says. Nancy feels the ropes tightly bound around her wrists and ankles as she lies in her bed. She has just woken up and is desperately trying to make sense of what is happening, her restraints getting seemingly tighter the more she struggles. She is screaming, but no sound is coming out. The sock Henry has stuffed in her mouth muffles her cri de coeur. She looks over at her husband, bound and gagged as she is, beside her.

Henry leaves the room quickly, looking back to check that his parents are still in position. The couple can do nothing but look at one another, fear and hope shifting between them. Jonathan looks at his wife and leans in, stretching the ropes that he is bound by, edging closer and closer to his wife. He rests his forehead upon hers, noses touching slightly. Jonathan stays in this position for as long as he possibly can, taking in every second until finally, he can hold no more, the restraints too strong, and he falls back to his side of the bed, the apparition of his son who had stood over him moments ago tormenting him.

Henry finally returns to his parents' room, but to Nancy and Jonathan's horror, he leads his two sisters into the room with him, both following behind, one in each of his hands, both in matching nighties and rubbing the sleep from their eyes. Tucked into Henry's belt is a knife. Nancy recognises it as one of hers from the kitchen, large, with a long wooden handle and extremely sharp. Henry stands at the end of the bed. Both girls are visibly petrified, frozen on the spot and unable to comprehend the situation going on around them. Confused and shocked, staring at their mum and dad, bound, and gagged, naked on the bed.

"Mum, something horrible is happening inside of me, and I don't know why."

Henry pauses for a second. He looks to the large bay window of the bedroom, gathering his thoughts. Emily and Sarah are frozen in terror, but unable to leave the brother they still trust despite the circumstances.

"Do you know the problem with that saying? You know the one, the one from Disney? From the movies? How does it go again, Sarah? What's the one I'm thinking of Emily? Ummm… Oh yes, that's it, 'May all your dreams come true.' Well! The problem is, Mum and Dad, the issue for me, the thing that I can't work out is, all my dreams are all nightmares, every single one. They are a succession of a different hell every time I close my eyes. They are people I meet, people I see in the street dying. I see their darkest secrets, an everlasting pit of despair and torture. If my dreams came true, this world would be reduced to fire and pain. It's something I can't control, and I know I have to come to peace with it now, but this is not a world I want to be a part of anymore."

Tears begin to roll down his face, and for a moment there is quiet, then without taking his eyes off his parents, in one very quick movement, he slits Sarah's throat. He did it as if he'd done it a thousand times before, taking the knife almost all the way to the back of her spine. Emily looks on in horror as her sister falls to the floor. Sarah twitches uncontrollably and sporadically as she falls to the carpet. Before Emily can even understand what has happened to her sister, Henry gently covers her mouth and repeats the process on his youngest sister. He holds her tightly. She struggles, but he embraces her until she is dead, and gently lays her on the floor next to Sarah.

In Emily's and Sarah's final embrace, they are facing each other, Sarah's arm placed on the side of her sister's head as if gently stroking her hair, and Emily's head nestled under her sister's chin. Nancy and Jonathan lie, stunned and horrified at what is unfolding. They are crying, helpless, minds racing, but both longing for their own turn with Henry, begging for it, longing for their end.

Henry takes a lighter out of his front pocket and a rag out of his back pocket. He sets the rag alight. Jonathan looks on at this, transfixed; the anger in his eyes as he stares at his son is palpable. Nancy lies on her back, sobbing uncontrollably. She stares at anything but her son and her two dead daughters. She feels a pain so severe, a pain so inexplicable she feels her body may burst. She then finally contorts her body up and sees her two daughters' legs lying motionless at the end of the bed. The carpet is a sea of blood, a red wave flowing outward to cover the bedroom floor.

Henry places the lit rag on Nancy's dressing table next to her perfumes, and the top immediately takes light. He then moves over to the window, careful not to step on his sisters' lifeless bodies. Henry then lights both floor-length linen curtains from the bottom and stands back. The flames immediately flash upward, spreading across the top to where they meet in the middle of the rail. The shape is what can only be described as an arch—a fiery gateway. Nancy looks over to see the silhouette of her son standing beneath this gateway into hell. He remains here for a while, staring through this portal he has created, into the corridor where he will surely descend.

Henry then returns to his parents' bed, again careful not to step on his lifeless sisters. He takes his knife from his belt and raises it. Nancy screams, and the sock becomes dislodged from her mouth. "Stop, Henry! Please!" Henry looks at her and pauses. Nancy can tell he is confused between the two boys she knows he is and can be. Henry looks at his sisters for a moment, contemplating his actions—why he is here, not just in this situation, but in this existence. Then he returns to that person who has just cut the throats of two small girls. He shoves the sock back into his mother's mouth and turns to face his father.

"You might think I hate you, Dad, but it's the opposite. You are my hero. You are perfection. You are this family, and I know I will never live up to you or become anything of the man you are, and I'm sorry I couldn't do that for you. I do love you, and I know none of this is your fault and I am… truly… truly… sorry, Dad." Jonathan then closes his eyes as he feels the blade pierce his chest and he knows this is the end. Jonathan's final and everlasting thoughts are of his family, all his family playing in their garden as he watches from his chair on the patio of their house, happy and content.

Nancy observes as her husband draws his last breath, her family departing this world, one by one, all around her. She leans into Jonathan, just to feel him one last time, her cheek pressed against his forehead. There, still feeling his warmth against her skin, she closes her eyes tightly and imagines he is still with her, just for a second. Nancy opens her eyes, bloodshot and weary. She looks at her son as he observes his devastation, the fire raging around him, sweat dripping from his brow. He is a shadow, emotionless, finally meeting his mother's eye.

She still loves him. It is not within her not to, despite what has happened and what he's done, she wants to be with her family. Nancy gently nods her head towards her son, indicating that this is her time. She lies back, waiting and longing for the final blow, for the ending she craves, but Henry is still and silent. He stares at his mum, looking into her, remembering, understanding why he has done this, why he has saved his family. He then brings his knife up and stops. He does this several times, full of intention but with no final action, an invisible force holding him back.

The flames now rise to the walls and ceiling, surrounding the room in a blaze, and smoke begins to enter their lungs. Henry's face shines from the sweat. He is like a porcelain doll, a singular petrified state, emotionless and hollow, until finally, he smiles at his mum, and he is alive, that smile that Nancy had adored from the first time she had seen it, that smile everyone loved.

"We were not the first, Mum, and we won't be the last, you will see as I have, don't suffer like me."

Henry takes the knife he is now twirling in his right hand. His last action is to raise the blood-soaked blade and slice his own throat, without a single flinch or hesitation. The movement is fluid and clean. He is still smiling at Nancy, at the mum who tried but could not help him, the mum who loved him through everything.

Henry falls to his knees, blood pouring from his mouth and neck. With his last strength, he crawls to the place where his sisters are at rest and holds them both, one arm over each of their bodies, as if he were protecting them from the fire and the evils of the world, covering their bodies with his own, and finally ending his life and his eternal torment.

Nancy lies on the bed, fire raging around her, smoke filling her lungs, hoping to die or to wake up from this nightmare. Was this real? What is happening? Reality escapes her and for a second, she doesn't truly know what is real. As her eyes close and she drifts away, just as the sleep finally comes, she sees a figure coming towards her. "Jonathan," she says under her breath. She feels strong arms wrap themselves around her, and her body elevated from her bed. When she opens her eyes, she is in a beautiful church. Her family are around her, glorious sunlight penetrating a large stained-glass window, the striking image of St Michael vanquishing the Devil before her, then nothing.

Chapter 18 – In The End

Nancy wakes abruptly. She is dazed and confused. She scans the room, trying to make sense of what's happening. "Where am I?" she mutters as her brain reconfigures, and the overwhelming brightness drains from her eyes. Her mind very suddenly becomes clear. She realises she is in her own bed, in her lovely bedroom, in her family home, her dressing table against the wall to her left, the antique armoire her grandmother had given her when she moved into her first flat next to the red upholstered chair, the one she and Jonathan had bought the day after they'd moved in, the linen curtains open and unscathed, her clothes from the previous day draped over the footboard and two dirty men's socks on the floor. She hears her husband downstairs noisily making breakfast and singing to Bob Marley on BBC Radio 2.

The morning sunbeams push through the large gap in her curtain; flakes of dust dance through the beams and disappear into the room. Nancy sits up and leans forward. She brings her palm to her mouth and breathes in deeply. She holds her breath, still slightly puzzled. "Was it a dream? It can't have been!" she thinks to herself. "Please, please let it be a dream," she whispers under her breath, then looks around again at her beautiful bedroom. "It was," she whispers, inhaling her relief, her heart still beating like a hummingbird.

Nancy then lies back down and touches her hard, swollen tummy. She is pregnant, about seven months. As she composes herself, she remembers the previous day. She was on maternity leave, and she had taken Emily and Henry to see their grandparents. With her arm outstretched, she touches some strands of soft hair. She sees her eight-year-old son lying next to her, stirring. He yawns and rubs his eyes with the back of his hands and then his forearm. Henry sees his mum looking down at him.

"Morning, Mummy," he chirps, resting his head on his palm. Nancy chokes slightly as she tries to stop herself crying. A few tears roll down her cheeks. Henry stands up on the bed, bouncing slightly, then immediately jumps into her arms. He hugs her tight. "Are you ok, Mummy?" he says into Nancy's ear. He strokes the hair over her ear to confirm his child-like concern for her.

"Yes, I'm fine, darling, just a bad dream that's all, an awful dream, but everything's ok now. Shall we go for breakfast? I can smell Daddy cooking something yummy."

Kitchen cloth over shoulder, clad in his dressing-gown, Jonathan addresses his wife. "Morning love, how did you sleep?" With a pan in one hand and a spatula in the other, he stands in the centre of the kitchen. The sun is shining directly on the spot where he has positioned himself. He is the angel of the kitchen; Nancy amusingly thinks to herself as he walks over to her and kisses her gently on the lips.

Henry follows her into the kitchen. "Mummy had a bad dream and now she's sad."

Jonathan looks towards his wife before picking up Henry and giving him a cuddle. "Everything ok, Nancy?" he says as he kisses his son on the neck, making him giggle.

She is still visibly upset, but quickly she manages to reassure him that she's fine. "I just had a bad dream, dear." She manages a smile, thinking how ridiculous she is for being so upset. "I'm 34 years old, for Christ's sake." She scratches her forehead and lets out an indeterminate laugh.

Jonathan is not convinced. "Are you sure you're ok?" he asks, disquieted.

"Yes, I'm fine. Now get me some breakfast." Nancy smiles and breathes deeply, this time allowing herself to feel the relief that she was fine, and her family was fine. She sits at the table and pours herself a coffee. Sarah looks at her mum from her highchair beside Nancy. "Hello, my beautiful girl." Sarah had been observing her parent's interaction with intrigue, but as a one-year-old, oblivious to the situation unfolding before her.

"Breakfast is served," sings Jonathan, as he dishes out sausages and beans to a now much more cheerful Nancy. "So, I may have done something naughty when I was out with Henry on Thursday, after we had finished at the park," Jonathan says to his wife, the tone preparing her for something, as a weary husband does occasionally. Nancy frowns with scepticism and stares at her mildly nervous husband. "Well, I blame Henry really, it's his fault for asking me." Henry smiles at his father, already knowing the news, and his father smiles back mischievously.

"What's going on, you two?" Nancy nervously asks her husband. "I'm not sure I'm in the mood for surprises today, to be honest."

Jonathan pulls out a photograph and places it hesitantly on the table in front of her. "This is the new addition to our family, Nance. He arrives on Tuesday. He just needs some jabs, and then he's all ours."

Nancy's stomach sinks and a bead of sweat materialises on her temple. A kitten playing with a small yellow ball, a ginger and white tabby. Nancy opens her mouth but is still silent.

"Are you mad at me, love? I thought you would be happy. to be honest. You said a while ago, maybe we should get a family pet. I remember, because we were at the café and you saw Jan and Ian from number 34, with their golden retriever, do you remember? That's when you said it!" Jonathan says, desperately trying to defend his actions. Before Nancy can answer, the phone rings. Once, then again and again. Jonathan waits a few seconds. He can see his wife is perplexed but finally gets up to answer the unrelenting rings. He walks to the hallway and picks up the telephone.

Nancy stays seated. She stares at the photo, the cat she already knows all too well. It was the cat from her dream. It was Pebbles, or was it? "Maybe not?" she muses softly to herself.

Nancy's attention is diverted from the perplexing photo of the cat. She hears a muffled Jonathan talking in the hall. He's concerned, his tone is solemn and sad, and Nancy's concentration is now fully focused on the call. "Ok, I'll get her now, Val, and again, I'm so, so sorry. If there's anything we can do, please don't hesitate to ask." Nancy hears Jonathan place the handpiece softly on the hallway table and walk slowly back, taking a moment before stepping into the kitchen. He looks directly at Nancy but says nothing. He is pale, and his eyes are beginning to well. He is the colour reserved for the most terrible of life's tragedies. He simply points to the phone and opens his mouth, unable to speak, then he leans back on the kitchen wall and slumps to the laminate floor, head in hands.

"What's happened, Jonathan? Tell me!" Nancy angrily asks her husband, already guessing what was said, but wishing and hoping she's wrong. "What has happened, Jonathan?" He shakes his head and tries desperately to hold back his tears. Nancy then gets up, walks to the door and stands for a second. The corridor is long, with dark wooden flooring; each step creaks as she makes her way to the phone. Nancy picks up the handpiece and brings it almost to her ear. "Please, Lord... please, Lord, this can't be happening," she whispers silently to herself, then finally puts the phone to her ear and breathes.

"She's dead, Nancy! Harriet's dead! My baby's dead!" Val's voice booms down the phone. The tone of her scream is enough to bring Nancy to her knees. With a thud, her legs hit the mahogany floor, the hollowness tightens in her stomach, and a pang of disbelief circulates her body.

"Fuck this life, fuck God! What child dies of a heart attack at 21?" Nancy immediately throws up onto the wall opposite her, changing the stone paint to a blood-like burgundy colour. She leans back on the wall. Val's cries are haunting and uncontrolled. Hearing her friend in pain, she attempts to regain some semblance of normality. Disregarding herself, her friend's daughter is dead, and Nancy would do anything to help. She pulls herself together. "Where are you, Val? I'm coming... I'm coming to you now! Where are you love?"

She pulls the drawers of the hallway table, trying to locate her car keys, frantically but unsuccessfully. She opens all the drawers, quickly, one by one, moving and throwing paperwork and objects aside, until the last one, which is full of drawings. Her eyes focus on the images below her. "No... no... no...! This can't be, who is doing this? What's happening to me?" There in the drawer are Margaret, Jayne, Debbie, and Bryson, her co-patients, each intricate detail the same as she remembered, every face like the ones from her dream, all her sketches placed one on top of the other in that bottom drawer. Nancy picks them up, her hand shaking uncontrollably. "I... I... I drew these, I remember, I remember, but where?" she looks intently at each one with disbelief. The sketch of Jayne slips from her hand and floats to the floor, her dark eyes steady as she falls, and even though this is just a drawing, she stares directly at Nancy.

Nancy is expressionless. The corridor is silent, apart from Val's faint cries emitting from the receiver of the phone. Nancy leans down to collect the sketch from the floor and notices someone. Henry is standing at the front door at the opposite end of the corridor. He stares at his mum, motionless and rigid, eyes wide and glazed, unblinking. Nancy stands to face her eight-year-old son. For a moment, they stare at each other trying to understand what was happening.

"Henry do... d... d... do you know what's happening? I can't under..." The breath escapes Nancy's lungs, and she can speak no further. She is petrified. She stares at her son, and he stares back. Tears start to roll from her eyes, but her face stays the same. Focusing on Henry's presence in front of her, she finds some air. "Please! Please, Henry!" A scream reverberates throughout the room. She becomes suddenly weak and once again falls to her knees, hands pressed against the cold floor, face down, sobbing, but only for a second. A strange feeling comes over her, and she summons the energy to look upward.

Henry is there now, standing over her, still rigid, eyes glazed. Nancy looks into her son's empty eyes. He gently tucks her hair behind her ear and rests his palm on her cheek. "I love you, Mummy; no one will ever love you as I do."

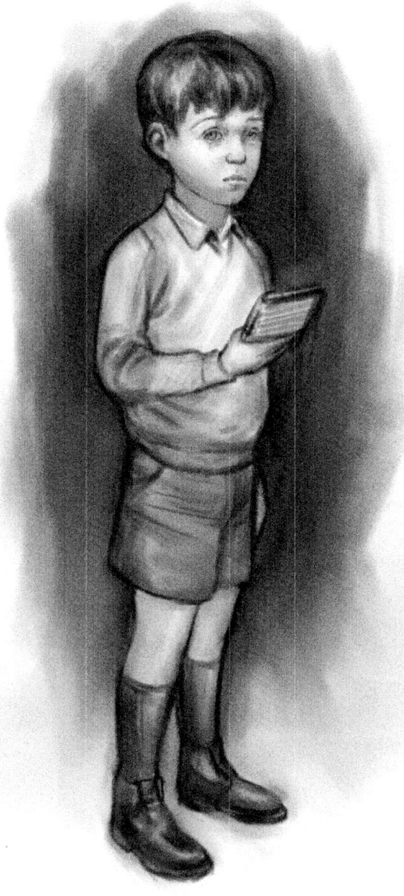

18 THE CRYING HOUR - APPENDIX

18.1 CHARACTERS:

Nancy Blake

Mary Kinnock—head nurse

Val—nurse and friend

Debbie Flint—patient

Jayne Cob—patient

Jonathan—husband

Sarah and Emily—the daughters

Henry—son

Bryson Collins—patient

Barry—patient

Mary—patient

Grace—mother

Grandmother—(nameless)

Mary—Nancy's second cousin and Grace's Cousin

18.2 TIMELINE

January 1955 – Father dies

February 1955 – Father's funeral

October 1965 – Nancy meets Jonathan.

June 1967 – Nancy finds her dream home with Jonathan.

November 1968 – Henry is born

October 1976 – the incident with Jonathan and Henry – eight years old

1979 – Margaret's funeral

Feb 1982 – the incident with the cat

July 1982 – Henry is collected from hospital—flashback of incident

March 1984 – the day in which the book is set

1984 – The revelation

The wake up